DOCTOR'S LEGACY

When Dr Helen Farley arrives in the Cornish fishing village of Tredporth as a locum, she feels instantly at home, and is fascinated by the large house standing on the cliffs. Owned by the ageing Edsel Ormond, her most important patient, the estate has two heirs: Howard and Fenton, Edsel's grandsons. But when Edsel informs Helen that he's decided to leave the property to Howard alone, on the condition that he first marries — and that the woman must be *her* — she realises her problems are only just beginning . . .

PHYLLIS MALLETT

◆

DOCTOR'S LEGACY

Complete and Unabridged

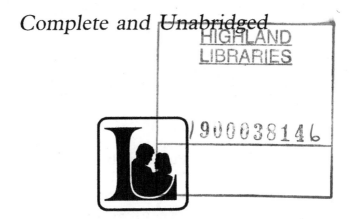

LINFORD
Leicester

First published in Great Britain in 1968

First Linford Edition
published 2019

A catalogue record for this book is available
from the British Library.

ISBN 978–1–4448–4195–4

Published by
F. A. Thorpe (Publishing)
Anstey, Leicestershire

Set by Words & Graphics Ltd.
Anstey, Leicestershire
Printed and bound in Great Britain by
T. J. International Ltd., Padstow, Cornwall

This book is printed on acid-free paper

1

Helen Farley began to grow excited as she walked faster along the narrow road. All her life she had dreamed of visiting Cornwall, to stand on the wind-swept cliffs and stare out over the rolling waves that beat ceaselessly against the high and obdurate rocks. The sound of the sea held a kind of magic for her, a sensation that was mixed inextricably with her dreams. She fancied that she could hear the sullen beat of the sea in the distance, but this was mid-June, and there was a heatwave at the moment, so there would be no ships wrecked in the jagged coves, and the smugglers would be well clear of the bays this afternoon.

She smiled at her romantic thoughts, and walked a little faster. Dressed in a pair of scanty pink shorts and a white blouse, she could feel the heat in the faint breeze, and her blonde hair stuck to her forehead in little damp curls. She narrowed her blue eyes as she stared ahead in an attempt to catch her first glimpse of the sea, but there was no horizon before her, and she could not tell if the deep blue low down was sea or sky.

The walk up from the village had been harder than she imagined. But from down below the sight of the lofty house standing in grand solitude on the cliff-top had attracted her from the moment she had arrived, and it seemed the very personification of all her romantic thoughts of Cornwall. If the present owners were not mixed up in smuggling, then she was certain their ancestors must have been. The house was still above her, but little more than half a mile away, and this winding road which had beckoned her on from the very moment she set foot out of the village seemed to wind on forever. But it was the sea she could hear in the distance, and Helen pushed forward with suppressed excitement in her, aching for her first glimpse of the deep water.

The road twisted sharply to the left, and Helen paused, glancing along it, for it had lost its diversity and now travelled straight along the cliff-top to the big house. A narrow footpath led straight ahead to the very edge of the cliffs, and there was a sign stating that it was prohibited for motor vehicles to use it. Helen agreed with that sign. The path could only be used by the smugglers and their ponies, or donkeys, whatever they had used to transport the contraband. She stood for a moment, listening intently to the muffled sound of waves beating against the foot of steep cliffs, and her imagination began to work overtime. Then she sighed and turned to study the big house. It came straight out of the pages of some period novel of these parts, she thought romantically. The tall chimneys atop the long, steep roofs, were like accusing fingers, and she was certain a lookout could have perched among them to watch for the appearance of the revenue-men. The many windows in the front of the building seemed blank in the bright sunlight, staring straight out to sea as if watching for the next storm to come in from the broad Atlantic. The atmosphere was thick on that hot afternoon.

The sound of a car door slamming brought Helen out of her reverie, and she looked around with something like irritation in her mind. Some people had no souls! The thought filtered through her as she spotted a small grey van parked on the verge. The figure coming towards her was of a woman dressed in fawn sports-shirt and blue jeans.

'Hello there,' the woman called. 'Are you alone?'

'I am,' Helen replied. 'Is anything wrong?'

'I can't get the van to start,' came the swift reply. 'I was hoping there was a man with you.' The woman came closer, and Helen guessed that she was about her own age, somewhere in the late-twenties. 'I suppose I shall have to walk up to the big house and use their telephone, but it will take the man from the garage an hour to get here, and I'm short of time as it is.'

'Perhaps there's something I can do,' Helen said with a smile.

'You know about cars?' The woman sounded surprised. 'I haven't the faintest idea what went wrong. It was going all right, and I'd just stopped to take a look at the sea — I can't resist it when I come up to the big house. Now I've tried to start it again and nothing happens. It's completely dead.'

She turned and walked back towards the van, and Helen went with her. She didn't stop talking, and didn't seem to expect an answer from Helen.

'Are you on holiday?' she demanded. 'Holiday-makers seem to come here earlier each year.'

'No, I'm not on holiday,' Helen replied. They reached the van and the woman slid behind the wheel and went through the motions of starting, but nothing happened. There was no response at all from the engine.

'What do you think?' the woman demanded anxiously, looking up at Helen. She had dark brown hair that ringed her face in a smart, tight style, and there was worry in her dark eyes.

'Let's lift the bonnet and try to find out,' Helen said.

'It's not out of petrol. I filled up on my way here.'

'It's not lack of petrol,' Helen agreed. 'The engine isn't even turning over, so it's to do with the battery or the start-motor, I imagine.'

The woman lifted the bonnet and peered at the display of mechanical precision revealed. Helen smiled as she bent over the hot interior. She checked the battery, and saw immediately that one of the leads was loose.

'Have you a screwdriver?' she asked.

'I think there's one in the toolbox.' The woman went to the rear of the van and rummaged for a few moments, then came back with the required tool.

Helen tightened the connection, then stepped back.

'Try it now,' she invited.

The woman shook her head dubiously, but got behind the wheel, and when she tried to start the engine it fired immediately. For a moment she sat there, staring at Helen in disbelief, and then she left the engine running and got out of the car.

'That was nothing short of a miracle,' she declared. 'Don't tell me you're a mechanic!'

'I'm a doctor,' Helen said with a musical laugh.

'A doctor! You're a very surprising person! If you're half as good with people as you are with engines then you must be a very good doctor indeed! You're strange to these parts, aren't you?'

'I am, but I hope to become a native in time. I'm acting as locum for Doctor Wyatt in Tredporth. He's going away for three months on account of his health, but he tells me that if I manage to settle in by his return I shall be offered a partnership. He was a very good friend of my father's a long time ago.'

'Then I hope you will settle in. My name is Margaret Bainter. I run a poodle parlour in Radmin, and do this country round every month or so. I'm on my way to the big house now. Can I give you a lift back to the village? You're a long way out.'

'I'm Helen Farley, and I walked up here to take a look at the sea. I haven't seen it yet, but if you're going to the house up there I'll look for you coming back.'

'I shall be about an hour,' Margaret Bainter said. 'I shall be delighted to run you back to Tredporth. I hope you'll like it around here. It's a bit quiet sometimes, but the holidaymakers will be coming soon, and you won't be able to move in the village.'

'I've been wanting to come down here for years,' Helen said. 'I hope I shan't be kept too busy to get around. I did spend some holidays at Dr. Wyatt's house a long time ago, but I've forgotten most of what I saw.'

'Perhaps I can see you sometime, and show you around,' Margaret Bainter said in friendly fashion. 'Apart from any other consideration, you're a very useful person to have around. How did you come to learn about the insides of cars? I should have thought it was hard enough to learn about the insides of humans.'

'I thought it would be wise to pick up a little knowledge. I'd hate to be called out to an urgent case in the middle of the night and find myself stuck on the roadside as you were.'

'Quite! Well I get a lot of driving done in a year, so it would be as well if I took a leaf from your book. I'll have to be going now, but I'll look for you on the way back. I mustn't be late at 'Oceanus'. Old Edsel Ormond would stop breathing if I was.'

'Edsel?' Helen enquired. 'That's a strange name.'

'It belongs to a strange man. That big house up there is called 'Oceanus'. I suppose it's apt, because it overlooks the sea. The estate belongs to Edsel Ormond. He's ailing. I expect you'll soon be visiting him, if you've taken over in the village. He suffers badly from asthma, and he's seventy-nine. I don't know how he manages to go on wheezing around that big place. Sometimes his face is purple, but he goes on and on.' Margaret Bainter sighed. 'I do run on so, but I must be going, Doctor. I'll look for you on my way back. Thank you for what you did.'

'It was nothing,' Helen replied. 'I'd like to ride back to the village with you, so I'll keep my eyes open. It was a longer walk up here than I imagined.'

'You do have a car?'

'Oh yes! But it was too nice today for driving.' Helen waited for the woman to drive on, and then she turned and followed the footpath to the cliff-top.

Coming to the edge of the land without warning, Helen felt her breath taken away by the panorama awaiting her. She swayed on the cliff-top, and stepped back quickly, gasping at the sheer exhilaration of having nothing but hundreds of feet of bright air beneath her, and far below, churning and seething in sullen fury, the sea was badgering the cliff-bottom. The sea was calm, swelling gently under the pressures that had built up many miles distant, in the open ocean, and here and there small black rocks broke the bright surface like old stumps of some deluged forest. Helen remained breathless, breathing deeply as she took in the wonder of it all, and her romantic self accepted it all with avid interest.

'You'd better step back from the edge,' a voice said politely. 'It's not very safe just there.'

Helen frowned as she peered around, seeing no-one, and then she realised that the voice had spoken from beneath her, and looking down, she saw the blur of a man's upturned face some twenty yards below. He was clinging to the cliff-face, and his teeth glinted in a slow smile as he saw her surprise.

'What on earth are you doing down there!' Helen was shocked. 'Are you all right?'

'Perfectly. Don't be alarmed. I'll be with you in a few minutes. But please stand back from the edge. A holiday-maker fell to his death from that spot last summer.'

Helen moved back instantly, and stood tensely awaiting the man's appearance. She heard and saw nothing until his head showed suddenly some yards to her left, and the next moment he had heaved himself upon firm ground and moved away from the edge. He came towards her with a smile on his tanned face, and she noted how brilliantly his teeth were gleaming in the sunlight.

'Sorry if I startled you a moment ago,' he said. 'But I saw that you were lost to the scene, and I feared that you might go over. It's very dangerous standing there if you're not used to it, and it wouldn't do for Tredporth to lose its new doctor before she had a chance to enjoy her visit.'

'You know who I am!' Helen accused.

'I do.' His brown eyes were filled with brightness as he studied her lovely face. When he glanced down at her brief shorts a smile came to his face. 'I don't think I've ever seen a prettier doctor, or one dressed so becomingly. I'll wager that your London patients never saw you like this.'

'I'm not on duty at the moment,' Helen replied, feeling slightly embarrassed by his candid gaze. He was strikingly handsome, and she judged his age to be around thirty. He was wearing a pair of brown trousers, and a brown shirt that was open at the neck. The sleeves of the shirt were tightly rolled, and his forearms and biceps were heavy. There was a shimmer of sweat on his forehead, and Helen thought he looked the perfect outdoor type.

'I'd better introduce myself,' he said.

'I'm Howard Ormond. I live at the house up there, and I know all about you because Grandfather Edsel has sworn that you'll never darken his doorway, emergencies notwithstanding. He's against women doctors on principle, and he swears that if Doctor Wyatt goes off and leaves him stranded he'll throw himself off the top of the cliff.' He paused and smiled. 'But I think he'll relent if he has one of his bad attacks. Have you been up to the house yet?'

'I haven't. I believe Dr. Wyatt is leaving it until just before he goes away. I've wondered why, but your words seem to explain it. However I am looking forward to seeing 'Oceanus'. It's captured my imagination somewhat, standing up here like a sentinel above the crags.'

'So you're a romantic as well!'

'How would you know?'

'Because that's exactly how I feel about the place, about the whole area,' he said complacently. 'It takes one romantic to recognise another.'

'I must plead guilty,' Helen said, smiling. She had taken an instant liking to him. She could picture him as a smuggler from the past, if he had been dressed for the part, and her imagination instantly supplied him with a woollen cap and turned-down thigh-boots and a horse-pistol stuck into a red sash tied around his lean waist.

'Well there are plenty of items in the house to take you back to more colourful days. But I must admit that I'm not a smuggler. I do nothing more eventful than run a small engineering firm in Radmin.'

'Perhaps your ancestors were smugglers, if they came from Cornwall,' Helen suggested with a smile.

'Very likely. The house has been in the family for generations. This present one was rebuilt on the site of the original. There are smuggler caves under the house, with secret doorways and all. If you are all that interested I shall be happy to show you around.

This ledge I just came along is a bolt-hole from the house.'

'Isn't it dangerous, climbing along the cliff-face with no rope?' Helen demanded.

'It's safe enough if you know the way, and have a head for heights,' he replied with a smile. 'I've been along that ledge a hundred times. The first time was when I was fourteen. It was a dare from my cousin Fenton. He lives at the house as well. But just listen to me running on!' He paused and smiled. 'I'm not really like that as a rule.' He turned and stared out to sea, his dark eyes narrowed against the glare of the sun.

Helen studied his sharp profile. He was a handsome man, and friendly. Was he married? The thought crossed her mind, and then he turned to her again, smiling, his face gentle.

'Would you like to come up to the house this afternoon?' he demanded impulsively. 'If you've got to meet my grandfather then there's no time like the present, and I should like to see his

16

face when he gets a look at you. It will save Dr. Wyatt the trouble of bringing you out, although he's very often up at the house. He gets along very well with Edsel.'

'I should love to come,' Helen said doubtfully, 'but will it be all right?'

'Of course. You don't want to believe too many of the stories you'll hear around the village about 'Oceanus'. It isn't haunted, and we're not smugglers any more.'

'It isn't that,' Helen said. 'I wouldn't want to intrude.'

'I'll introduce you as a friend of mine,' he replied. 'I presume this is your day off, and it's mine, at least the afternoon and evening on a Friday is my only concession to relaxation. I have been at a loose end until now. If you are just looking around then I'll be glad to put myself at your disposal as a guide. Being a doctor, you'll need to know where everyone lives, especially the people who don't live in the village.'

'If you're sure it's no trouble,' Helen

said, still doubtful.

'A golden rule is always be nice to doctors,' he said with a smile. 'You never know when you'll need their professional advice or skill. I was in the Boy Scouts as a youngster, and I haven't forgotten the old rule about one good deed every day. I don't often get the opportunity of doing good deeds nowadays, so don't deny me the chance when it arises.'

'All right.' Helen was smiling. She liked his manner. He wasn't like a stranger, and he seemed keen to have her company. That must mean that he wasn't married, and she couldn't understand why such a handsome man should remain unattached.

'We'll walk up to the house by way of the road,' he suggested. 'I don't think I'll trust you to the ledge.'

'I'm afraid I'm no good at heights,' Helen said with a shudder. 'I got such a strange feeling when I looked down at the sea.'

'It's something you can get used to,'

he replied. 'Now Fenton is afraid of heights. He dared me to go along that ledge when I was fourteen, and I did it. But he's never done it, and I don't suppose he ever will. Fenton is my cousin, I think I mentioned. His father and my father were brothers.' They began to walk along the path to the road as he spoke. 'His father was the eldest, and was drowned in the sea just below the house. There is a spot on the cliff-top called *Fool's Leap*. It takes a brave man as well as a fool to dive into the sea from that point, and Fenton's father did it. I sometimes think that's why Fenton is like he is. My father was killed in the war. My mother died of a broken heart.'

They walked along the road, and Helen listened intently to his words. When they approached tall, black iron gates that stretched right across the road he paused, and Helen stared at the house through the bars of the gate. The building was old, and creeper clung to the south walls, but there was none on the east side. There was a brooding atmosphere about it, Helen decided. She felt her heartbeats quicken as Howard Ormond opened a small gate and ushered her into the grounds.

'Don't take any notice of Edsel's harsh manner,' he said as they walked along the driveway to the house. 'His bark is worse than his bite. He might snap at you, but I don't think he ever means it. A lot of people are afraid of him, but I've always found him kind and generous.'

The sound of barking dogs attracted Helen's attention, and Howard Ormond laughed.

'They're Fenton's animals,' he said. 'Fenton is the local vet. I can never understand why he took to it, because there's a cruel streak in him. At least there was when I was a youngster. He's several years older than me, and I used to get hell from him before I was big enough to fight back.' He smiled, and Helen admired his profile as he stared at the house in front of them.

'You're extremely fortunate to be living in such exquisite surroundings,' she said as they approached the front steps. The house was even larger than it had seemed from a distance, and it had stark lines that conveyed a chill atmosphere even in the heat wave. It was as if the cold winds and storms of the winters it had experienced had permeated the very brickwork for all time, resisting the warmth of summer, exuding strange dankness in order to ward off heat and life.

Helen noticed that all the windows in the front of the house were closed, and the dark curtains were still and lifeless, instead of fluttering in the warm breeze that came off the sea. She had a sudden feeling of stifling and, despite the deep breath which she took as Howard Ormond opened the thick black door, the feeling of oppressiveness stayed with her.

'I don't suppose it will go on much longer,' he muttered. 'When Edsel dies there will be a lot of trouble over the estate. I'm not bothered about it for myself, but Fenton has been dropping hints for years that he's the son of the eldest son, and as such he should have the lion's share. I'm not saying that I don't want any part of it, but my reasons are different. Fenton is concerned only with the property and the money. I'm not that interested. My business — that was my father's business — is doing very well, and it's because of my father's memory that I'd like to get this place. Fenton's father didn't care about anything. They say he was insane when he dived into the sea, because Fenton's mother had gone off with a stranger from London, some artist who was painting the local scenery.'

He broke off as they crossed the threshold, and Helen saw that his face was set in harsh lines. But when he caught her eye he smiled.

'I must apologise,' he said. 'I don't know why I should be running on to you like this. Perhaps it's because you're a doctor as well as a woman. That makes you something more than a mere female.'

'Thank you,' Helen replied lightly. 'Although I don't know if that is a compliment or not.'

He laughed loudly as they paused in the wide hall. Helen looked around with great interest. There was plenty of space in this old house. The hall ran straight through to the back of the house, and there were twin staircases rising broadly on either side, turning inwards to meet and join at the first storey. What furniture stood in the hall was old and dark, and again Helen felt the sensation of stifling. When she took a deep, audible breath Howard Ormond laughed.

'It is a bit heavy in here,' he admitted. 'I know just how you feel. This place always caught me like that when I first came here to live. I've got used to it now. It's the air, I suppose. Edsel suffers from cardiac asthma, and although Dr. Wyatt tells him to get plenty of fresh air he won't have a window opened anywhere. He never leaves the house now.'

'Then you should try and educate him in the ways of helping his health,' Helen said firmly.

'I hope you're not going to try and do that.' Dark eyes regarded Helen with interest. 'Dr. Wyatt gave it up as a bad job. You don't know Edsel! But I'd like to see you try. A woman might have more chance of success, and poor old Edsel could do with a helping hand. But come along and meet him. I expect he's awake now. I see the poodle-woman is here, and Edsel likes to watch the dog being clipped.'

Helen wondered what she had let herself in for as she followed Howard Ormond along the hall and into the library. Dr. Wyatt had told her some-thing of his most influential patient, and it all came back to her as she prepared to meet him. There were a lot of tales circulating the village about 'Oceanus' and the Ormonds, and she was intrigued to find out truth from fiction.

2

The old man seated in the big chair by the empty fireplace was tall and thin, with a pale, unhealthy face and burning brown eyes. He looked at Helen lifelessly, his gnarled hands resting like dead branches upon the arms of the dark-stained chair. For a moment Helen thought he was asleep with his eyes open, so motionless he remained, and she glanced at the busy figure of Margaret Bainter, seated at the mahogany table on which stood a white poodle.

'Ignore the dog.' The old man's voice cracked harshly in the dry, hot atmosphere, and Helen glanced towards the tall windows at the far end of the room. They were tightly closed, and the air was musty and stale. A good stiff sea breeze blowing in through every window in the house would have been hard put to remove the taint of old age, Helen thought.

'Grandfather, this is Dr. Helen Farley,' Howard Ormond said. 'She was admiring the outside of the house, and I thought it as well to bring her in. When Dr. Wyatt goes away she will be attending you, and she ought to know you before she has to come professionally.'

'A woman doctor!' The old man stirred impatiently. 'I told Wyatt he was a damned fool. This isn't London. The men hereabouts have more pride. I wouldn't let a woman touch me.'

'I think you would if you had one of your bad attacks,' Howard said, smiling at Helen. 'She's a qualified doctor, and as such she deserves a little respect.'

'I welcome her to my house as a visitor, but not as a doctor,' old Edsel Ormond said, sitting up slowly and stiffening his narrow shoulders. 'How do you do, Doctor? So you like 'Oceanus', do you?'

'I think it's enchanting, Mr. Ormond,' she replied lightly.

'I think so, too,' the old man said

drily. 'Offer her a drink, Howard. I suppose you've been climbing along that wretched ledge again. One of these days you're going to make a mistake.'

'You're jealous, Grandfather!' the younger man retorted. 'In your youth you made that climb a hundred times.'

'True, but not after I grew to manhood and found my senses. But the Ormonds aren't the same any more. I was the last true Ormond. The family is too old now. I think it's a good thing that you and Fenton haven't married. The blood is tired.' Edsel Ormond spoke in a thin voice, and his breath wheezed in his chest. Helen knew the sound well, and she didn't like it. But the old man's dark eyes were upon her face, and there was a glint in them that did not escape her notice. 'What do you think of that as a medical person, Doctor?'

'I disagree with you,' she replied spiritedly, and Howard Ormond laughed heartily.

'You won't get your own way with

her as you've done with old Wyatt,' he observed. 'It's about time someone stood up to you. Perhaps she'll be able to make you feel better.'

'Not if I have to follow a lot of tiresome orders,' the old man said firmly. He didn't let his gaze wander from Helen's face. 'Anyway, I don't wish to discuss my health. I'll send for the doctor when I feel that I need her.'

'Would you care for a drink, Doctor?' Howard demanded. He studied her tall figure, and Helen suddenly became aware that she was dressed in brief shorts, and knew a pang of embarrassment.

'Really, I think I should be going,' she said. 'I'm not dressed for visiting. I was just walking around to get my bearings and to admire the views. My father told me a lot about this part of the country, and apart from the time I came to stay at Dr. Wyatt's as a girl I haven't been this way.'

'Your father was a local man?' Edsel demanded.

'Yes. He was born in Radmin. He and Dr. Wyatt were very close friends in their youth.'

'Would you have known him, Grandfather?' Howard Ormond demanded.

'I prided myself that once I knew every man who lived within fifty miles of this place,' the old man retorted. 'If he was a friend of Wyatt then I suppose I knew him. Wyatt brought a lot of his friends here.'

'He was a doctor also,' Helen said. 'He's dead now.'

'I'll talk to Wyatt about it,' Edsel promised. 'If I knew your father then it would help me to accept your attention in Wyatt's absence.'

Howard caught Helen's eye and smiled knowingly. He moved to a sideboard and produced bottles and glasses, but Helen declined a drink, and he put them away again.

'Grandfather doesn't drink,' he said, standing beside the old man's chair. He gazed fondly at Edsel Ormond, who snorted impatiently.

'Why aren't you at the factory, Howard?' the old man demanded. 'I don't know what's come to the younger generations. It was bad enough in your father's time, but grandchildren are even worse.'

'It's my afternoon off, and you well know it,' Howard retorted. 'Don't tell me that in your time you never took time off!'

'Well an afternoon here and there, but there was usually paper-work at home to be done. Business was a damned sight harder in those days, Howard.'

'I'm sure it was.' The younger man was smiling. 'Do you mind if I take Dr. Farley and show her over the house?'

'Do so by all means.' Edsel was still staring at Helen. 'Perhaps you'd do me the kindness of calling one afternoon next week to talk with me, Doctor.'

'I shall be delighted,' Helen replied, feeling a little surprised. 'Any particular afternoon?'

'No. My time is my own now. I'm an

old man and of not much use to anyone these days. I sit around all day and every day. There's no help in me now. I expect you're rather busy at this time, however, so drop in when you find the time. It won't inconvenience me.'

'Are you feeling all right, Grandfather?' Howard demanded.

'As well as I shall ever feel before I go to my grave,' the old man retorted sharply. 'You leave my health to me, Howard.'

'Certainly. But I can't help wondering. You've been going on against Doctor Farley ever since Wyatt told you she was coming. But in the first few minutes of meeting her you change your mind.' He glanced at Helen and smiled broadly. 'I expect it's your charm that's wrought the change.'

'Take her along now, will you?' Edsel said firmly. 'The dog is becoming fractious, and Miss Bainter has a lot to do.' He studied Helen's face for a moment. 'It's been nice meeting you, Doctor. I will say that you are an improvement on old Wyatt. I expect your methods and treatments are more up to date than an old man's, but some of the old fashioned remedies are still the best.'

'Fresh air is an old fashioned remedy for the more distressing symptoms of your complaint,' Helen reminded gently. 'I suggest you open some of the windows and get rid of this stale atmosphere.'

There was a short silence, and Howard's expression showed that he thought Helen had said the wrong thing. But Edsel let his harsh expression break for a moment, and he smiled.

'Perhaps you're right,' the old man mused aloud. 'Howard, see that Lucy opens all the windows during the day, an hour before noon until an hour after.'

'Gladly, Grandfather,' Howard replied, moving towards the door. His face was showing the surprise that Helen was feeling. 'Come along, Doctor, and I'll be pleased to show you around.'

'Will you want that lift back to the

village, Doctor?' Margaret Bainter spoke for the first time, and Helen turned to smile at the woman.

'I'll be happy to drive the doctor back to the village later,' Howard said quickly. 'Perhaps I can prevail upon you to stay for tea, Doctor.'

Again Helen glanced down at herself. 'I'm not dressed for it,' she said uncertainly.

'I'll drive you to the village so you can change,' he said.

'Yes,' Edsel interrupted. 'Perhaps you'd like to do that, Doctor. If I'm to put myself in your hands for the three months that Wyatt will be away then I want to get to know you.'

'Very well,' Helen said. 'I'm sure it will ease Dr. Wyatt's mind if he can depart without having to worry about your welfare, Mr. Ormond. He has confided to me that you are the main source of his worries among his patients.'

'I can quite believe that,' Howard said with a smile, and Edsel Ormond shook his head.

'I don't worry anyone any longer,' he said tightly. 'I shall expect to see you later, Doctor.'

Howard escorted her from the room, and after he had closel the door he relaxed slightly and smiled at Helen.

'I don't know how you've managed it,' he said with a little wonder in his voice, 'but you've got him almost eating out of your hand already. Keep up the good work. There's a lot could be done to ease his condition, but he just won't go along with the doctor's orders. Fancy him agreeing to have the windows opened! Poor old Dr. Wyatt is always preaching that subject when he's here, and he doesn't get anywhere.'

'Then I must do all I can to gain your grandfather's confidence,' Helen said. 'Once that's been accomplished the rest will be easy. But does he have many attacks?'

'They come quite frequently, and they're most distressing,' Howard said. 'But I don't have to tell you that, do I?' He smiled as he led Helen towards the door. 'I'd better run you home first to enable you to change, and when we come back you can look over the house.'

'I shall look forward to that,' Helen said eagerly.

They left the house and walked around to a rear garage. Howard asked her to wait while he entered to bring out a gleaming black Bentley. When Helen got into the car at his side she exclaimed with delight, and he glanced sidelong at her and smiled.

'This makes my old car an apology for road transport,' she commented as he drove towards the large iron gates.

'It's the only luxury I have permitted myself,' he said. 'But I do like a good car. The trouble is I never go very far in it. Seems a waste to have it standing around gathering dust and rust.'

'It doesn't look very dusty or rusty,' Helen commented gaily, and they both laughed.

'When you get settled into your routine after Dr. Wyatt has gone and you know when you get some free time perhaps you'd care to come for a drive with me on the odd evening,' he said thinly. 'We lead Spartan lives at 'Oceanus' partly because of Grandfather's complaint, and partly because the old man is made that way. He's as hard as iron. He would have died a long time ago but for that.'

'He does look remarkably fit for his age, considering the complaint,' Helen agreed. 'It must have something to do with his surroundings. I should imagine that the house is a grim place in Winter. It has an atmosphere about it. I shouldn't be surprised to learn that it has the odd ghost or two.'

'Well I haven't met any in all the time I've lived there,' Howard said. 'I'm thirty now, and I came here to live when I was about five, so you see that I speak with some experience behind me. But you're quite right. It's a frightening place in Winter for any stranger. I've got used to all the odd noises, and I like nothing better on a stormy afternoon to get up into the attic and watch the sea from there. It's a sight to see, I can tell you. If you're still in these parts when the weather changes then you really must come up to the attic for a look.'

He halted the car just before the gates, and alighted to open them. As he walked back to the car another vehicle appeared along the road and came very fast towards them. When he saw it, Howard took a deep breath.

'Oh Lord!' he said quietly. 'Here comes Julia Anslow. This girl is a real menace on the road and in any man's company. She's makes up to me whenever she can, and plays up to Fenton. I believe her motives are 'Oceanus'. She doesn't know which one of us is going to inherit, and she's keeping us both in mind, ready to accept the heir.'

The car arrived so swiftly that Helen was unable to pass any comment, but she gazed with interest at the slim figure in the sports car. It was an open-top type, and the girl's long

37

blonde hair was picturesquely disarrayed over her head and shoulders like a golden veil that had come undone. She smiled at Howard, and subjected Helen to a close and narrow-eyed scrutiny.

'Hello there,' she greeted buoyantly. 'I was on my way to see you, Howard.'

'Sorry I'm not available this afternoon,' he replied easily. 'This is Doctor Helen Farley, who's taking Doctor Wyatt's place while he's away. Doctor, meet Julia Anslow.'

'How do you do?' the girl said formally, and Helen replied in similar tones.

'You will excuse us, Julia,' Howard said, still smiling. 'The doctor has been asked back to tea, and I'm driving her into the village so she can prepare herself for the ordeal.'

'Then you must have made a good impression, Doctor,' the girl said in careful tones. Her voice was sharp and taut, as if she had difficulty in preventing open hatred from sounding, and Helen wondered at that as she watched the girl's beautiful but distant face. 'So I'm to be stood up this afternoon, am I?' She watched Howard's face with calculating eyes.

'I wasn't aware that I had made any arrangements to see you, Julia,' he replied.

'Of course you didn't! You never do! But you're always at home on Friday afternoons, aren't you?'

'Except today.' He was smiling still, but his voice had an edge to it, and Helen could not help wondering what relationship existed between them.

'Is Fenton at home?' There was a trace of impatience now in the modulated voice.

'Not at the moment, but you are free to go up to the house and wait for him.' There was amusement seeping into Howard's tones. 'Grandfather is there, and he'd welcome your company.'

'You know he hates the very sight of me,' the girl retorted. 'I'll wait in the car outside until Fenton shows up. Will he be very long, do you think?'

'I'm afraid I can't say. No-one knows Fenton's movements. He may be away until after midnight, and then he might be coming home in a few moments.'

'All right. Don't let me delay you.' Julia Anslow stared at Helen for a moment, then started her car and went roaring along the drive towards the house.

'That's Julia, that was,' Howard said, driving out to the road and stopping to go back and shut the gates. 'I don't like her motives. She's a nice enough girl, and at one time I might have been taken in by her, if she hadn't let her manner convey so much of her feelings. But she's a gold-digger! Her father is Colonel Anslow, a retired military man who has a large estate along the coast a few miles. But they lack money, and that's what the Ormonds have an abundance of. The colonel wants his daughter to marry the man who inherits 'Oceanus', and he doesn't hide the fact half as well as Julia, who is a bad actress.'

Shutting the gates, he came back and they resumed the drive to the village. Helen sat back and enjoyed the scenery and the luxury of the car. Her mind was filled with many impressions and sensations gained that afternoon, and she felt as if she had been riding a merry-go-round. It was exhilarating, after so many dreary months of working in London. She had been hoping to get a change of scenery ever since her friendship with Gary Milton had fallen through, and although this locum job was only temporary, it had enabled her to get out of the rut, and during the next three months she would have the opportunity of considering her future.

'I suppose you're thinking that we're a very strange lot at 'Oceanus',' Howard said suddenly, and Helen jerked herself from her thoughts and glanced at him. His dark hair was low over his forehead in two rebellious waves, and his brown eyes were gleaming as they surveyed her.

'I wouldn't say strange,' she replied

warmly. 'You certainly have very romantic and extraordinary surroundings.'

'That's right, play it cautiously,' he
remarked, and then they were driving
into the little village.

Tredporth lay at the foot of cliffs that
swept back and upwards away from the
sea, and the cottages and houses were
huddled together in a straggly line
along the stone quay that kept the sea
in its proper place. Wooden jetties stuck
out into the bright water at intervals
along the quay, and Helen never tired
of watching the small boats in the
bay. They were so colourful, and the
fishermen were solid men who worked
hard out there in the open at their
arduous livelihood. In Summer they
didn't fish so much, but carried loads of
gay holidaymakers out and around the
bay. In Winter, when the sea permitted,
they went fishing, and Helen could
imagine the chill difference between the
two seasons. Now like a millpond, the
sea would change colour and mood,
and the men in their tiny craft would

have to beware of treachery and run for cover at the first sign of trouble. But they were seafaring men whose ancestors had depended more implicitly upon the deep waters for their precarious living, and experience through the generations had built up an instinct among these hardy people.

The doctor's house lay at the far end of the seafront, and Howard Ormond brought his big car to a halt before the little whitewashed gate. He switched off the engine and turned to Helen.

'I'll give you twenty minutes,' he said. 'I'll leave the car here. There's a person I want to see, and bringing you home has given me the opportunity of handling some business.'

'Thank you,' Helen said, and they both got out of the car. 'I'll be ready when you get back.'

'Take your time,' he responded with a smile. 'It's a woman's privilege to keep a man waiting.'

She opened the gate and passed through, and turned to watch his tall, broad-shouldered figure going along the quay. Her blue eyes narrowed as her thoughts raced, and when she turned to go into the house she told herself that if she saw Howard Ormond at all during her three months here in Cornwall then she should not lack interest. He was a most engaging man, and her curiosity about the whole family had been aroused by her brief visit to 'Oceanus' . . .

Entering the house, she saw the door of Doctor Wyatt's study standing open, and tapping at the door she heard Wyatt's strong voice asking her to enter. She went in, and her heart seemed to be beating faster than normal. It had been an unusual twist to her afternoon's outing, and one that she hadn't allowed for, but 'Oceanus' loomed large in her mind, and some of its mystifying atmosphere seemed to have entered her thoughts.

Russell Wyatt smiled when he saw her, and Helen began explaining the events of her afternoon. Wyatt was a stocky man, his short figure bearing some overweight. He was in his early sixties, with a wrinkled face and kindly blue eyes. He was like a father to Helen, and his voice was warm and gentle when he spoke.

'Helen, I'm so relieved!' he said. 'I've been worried about old Edsel up there in that big house. But you've made more progress in a few minutes than I've accomplished in all my life. He's a hard man to get close to, and I've never won his confidence. It's a distressing complaint which bothers him, and he's a headstrong man. He has ideas of his own, and won't change them. But perhaps you'll be able to make him more amenable in my absence. There's no reason why he shouldn't live for another ten years.'

'He's seventy-nine! That's a wonderful age in itself, but with his complaint it's almost miraculous.'

'He won't die.' Dr. Wyatt was happy. 'I've never come across a man with such an iron constitution. He's headstrong and wilful, just like a child, but I like him. You've met the better one of the two grandsons, too. Howard is all right. He has always kept himself to himself — not like Fenton. But of course their fathers were totally different, not like brothers at all. Fenton's father had a touch of insanity, you know. He had meningitis as a child, and it left him affected. That's a bit of professional confidence, by the way, and I'm not saying that Fenton is similarly affected, but I have room for doubting his reasons sometimes. He's the local vet, and I'll never know why he chose that profession. He was cruel as a boy.'

Helen was thinking that Howard Ormond had told her just about the same thing, and she wondered about Fenton Ormond. She turned to the door.

'I'll have to hurry,' she confided. 'Howard will be returning for me in about fifteen minutes.'

'Don't keep him waiting, my dear, and have a nice time. You must take things easy until I leave, and that's only ten days away. Have you told Edsel Ormond who your father is?'

'Did he know Father?' Helen demanded.

'When you go back to 'Oceanus' ask Edsel if he remembers the young doctor who set his leg when it was broken. I expect that will jog his long memory.'

'Was it Father?'

'Yes. Those were the good old days!' Wyatt sighed and shook his head. 'But don't let me start reminiscing, my girl, or you'll be here for the rest of the day. Off you go, and enjoy yourself.'

Helen went up to her room to change, and her thoughts moved swiftly as she did so. There was something about 'Oceanus' and the people who lived in it, she told herself remotely. In the darker confines of her subconscious mind her instincts and her intuition were at work, and she gained the impression that the next three months of her life would be the most significant and important ever. She dressed carefully, one eye on the time, and there was a sense of anticipation billowing up inside her as she finally left the room to go down to meet Howard Ormond. She felt instinctively that she had reached a turning point in her life as well as in her career. She had been at the crossroads ever since she had split up with Gary Milton, and Fate had held her in abeyance just for this moment. She was going down to meet Howard Ormond, and it might be the most fateful step she ever took!

3

Helen liked the admiration which shone in Howard Ormond's eyes when she left the house to find him waiting by the car. He nodded approvingly at her flowered skirt and white blouse, and she wondered at the emotion which spurted to life inside her as he opened the car door for her and helped her into the vehicle. He was a year older than she, the thoughts ran, and he was not actively interested in any woman. A picture of Julia Anslow came into her mind, and she wondered about the girl. Julia was a beautiful girl, and she was intent upon marrying well. But if Howard inherited 'Oceanus' upon his grandfather's death the girl would be disappointed, because Helen realised from Howard's remarks earlier that he had no illusions about Julia Anslow.

'I didn't ask because it never crossed

my mind,' Howard said as he drove back towards 'Oceanus', 'but is there a husband or a fiancé in the background. I asked you out, not realising that I might be laying myself open to an attack from an angry rival.'

'There's no-one,' Helen said, and felt a fluttering of nerves in her throat.

'Well that makes it simple. I don't have to go back on my offer, and you don't have to refuse.' He fell silent, and remained so until they were at the gates of the estate. When he halted to get out of the car he glanced at Helen, and there was a seriousness in his voice that she hadn't heard before. 'I don't want to sound loose-mouthed,' he said briefly, 'but I'd like to warn you about Fenton. Don't let his manner upset you if he's in one of his moods when we see him. He's morose at times, and sullen. Of course he may not show that side of his nature to you, but if he does then make allowances, will you?'

'Certainly,' she replied, and watched him opening the gates. She felt intrigued, and there was a sense of mounting excitement in her mind as he drove on to the house.

Howard left the car at the steps, and lost no time in showing Helen into the house. He took her on an immediate tour of the building, and Helen found that her flights of fancy concerning the place were not too far out. It was an interesting house, but she could not but help noticing that it was falling into decay. She wondered at it, and when they were at last mounting to the attic, Howard spoke of the general state of repair.

'Edsel won't spend a penny on the place,' he said heavily.

'Each time I mention it to him he tells me to wait until he's dead and gone before making plans. He seems to think that his heir should do the worrying about repairs, and he likes to joke now and again about which of us will inherit. It doesn't matter to me. I have quite enough with the business interests left by my father, but it's a touchy subject with Fenton, and sometimes there are the most dreadful rows between Fenton and Grandfather. Fenton can never see that Grandfather is just amusing himself at his expense. However I'd better not tell you all the family foibles or you'll begin to think that we're a queer lot indeed! This is the attic, and I'm sure you'll think it's the most important room in the house. The windows overlook the sea, and the sights that are visible from here in the height of a storm are indescribable.'

He led her into a long and wide room that had large windows like an artist's studio. There was a carpet on the floor, and a few items of dark furniture. It was obvious that at some time or other the attic had been used as a living room. They walked to the windows, and Helen felt breathless as she gazed out over the wide expanse of calm bright sea. She could imagine it instantly as it would be in a storm, and to her ears came the sound of blustering wind and roaring waves. She realised that Howard was watching her closely, with a half-smile upon his lips, and she nodded.

'It certainly stirs the imagination,' she said.

'I know just how you feel,' he commented, glancing at his watch. 'It's an awesome sight, I can tell you, and if you don't manage to see a storm while you're here then I suggest you come down as soon as the weather forecast indicates one. I give you a standing invitation to call on us whenever there's a bad storm.'

'I shall keep you to that,' Helen said with a smile.

'Now let's go and see if Edsel wants tea.' Howard led the way down to the lower parts of the house. He paused on the first floor landing, where the staircase split to make two separate descents to the ground floor. 'Julia's car wasn't out front when we came back, so I suppose she got tired of waiting for Fenton. I'm glad. I'd rather have tea quietly with a mellow grandfather than having him upset by either Fenton or

53

Julia. They both seem to rub him up the wrong way.'

When they reached the ground floor Helen told him how wonderful she thought the house was, and he smiled.

'Come and look into the kitchen,' he invited. 'I expect Lucy and Mrs. Sperry are busy with tea. Lucy is the maid, and Mrs. Sperry is the housekeeper. Ellen's husband, David Sperry, is the gardener and odd-job man.'

He led the way to the rear of the house and pushed open a door that gave access to a large and bright kitchen. A tall girl, dressed in a short black frock and a white apron, looked up from a book she was reading, and she turned swiftly when she recognised Howard and threw the book on to a table.

'Hello, Lucy,' Howard said. 'Is Mrs. Sperry about?'

'She's gone out into the kitchen garden to see Mr. Sperry,' the girl retorted. 'Is there anything I can do?'

'No. I'm just showing Doctor Farley

around the house. This is Lucy Southern, Doctor.'

The girl smiled, and Helen spoke to her. Howard went to the back door and opened it, peering outside before inviting Helen to follow him. They went out into a large garden, and Helen saw two people, a man and a woman, at the far end.

'Mr. and Mrs. Sperry,' Howard said. 'They're a good couple, and they've been here for as many years as I can remember.' He lifted a hand and waved cheerily when the woman turned to glance at them, and she replied in similar manner. 'I get on quite well with them, myself, but they hate the sight of Fenton.' He fell silent, and then shook his head. 'I don't know, Doctor,' he said slowly. 'I hope I'm not giving you a bad impression of Fenton. But everything I say about him isn't very good, is it? I've only just noticed it myself. There's a moral there somewhere. Perhaps Fenton should begin to look at himself, or I ought to guard my tongue.'

They went back into the house, and Howard ushered her into the library. Edsel Ormond was seated in a chair by the window, and he glanced around at them when he heard their entrance.

'Is tea ready?' he demanded irritably. 'We haven't been waiting for you to return, have we?'

'No, Grandfather. We've been here quite some time. I've shown the doctor all over the house. Would you like me to ring for Lucy?'

'Help me into the dining room first,' Edsel said, and Howard went to the old man's side and took an elbow. It was then Helen saw that Edsel Ormond used a stick to get around. He gripped a silver-topped cane with a gnarled hand and pushed himself erect, staggering a little as he took his first steps. He studied Helen's face as he came towards her, and there was the suspicion of a smile about his thin lips. He was taller than she had imagined, and he was also incredibly thin.

'What do you think of my home?' he

demanded, pausing in front of her.

'Most interesting,' Helen replied with fervour. 'It must be a wonderful place to live in.'

'It must have been, once,' he replied. 'Come along, my dear, and we'll rouse out the servants. It's time for tea.'

They went into the dining room, and when Howard had seated his grandfather he went off to the kitchen. Helen sat down on Edsel Ormond's right, for the old man pointed to the seat, and she was aware that his dark eyes were scrutinising her features. She glanced at him, and smiled.

'Doctor Wyatt tells me that you do, or did, know my father a long time ago,' she remarked.

'Really? I can't recall the name. What were the circumstances of our meeting?'

'You had broken your leg, and my father set it for you.'

'You need say no more. I have never forgotten that unfortunate incident. So that young doctor was your father!

That's strange, because I have often wondered since that day just how he fared in life.'

'He's dead now,' Helen said. 'He died a few years ago.'

'I'm sorry about that,' he said. 'And your mother?'

'She remarried two years ago, and lives in London. I don't see much of her nowadays.'

'I see. Well it's a small world, isn't it? Your father had very gentle hands, as I remember. And you say he came from these parts?'

'He was born in Radmin. My grand-father was the vicar of the parish church.'

'Of course! That's where I've heard the name mentioned. Farley. That's it. I have been wrestling with my memory since you first came. I don't forget many things, I can tell you, and at the mention of your name there was a ticking in my brain.'

Howard returned, and glanced anxiously from Helen to his grandfather. Helen smiled reassuringly, and Howard nodded and smiled.

'This girl is a local woman,' Edsel Ormond remarked as Howard sat down opposite Helen. 'She was just telling me about her father and grandfather.' He related the facts as Helen had given them. 'I don't know why locals want to drift away from their birthplaces,' he ended.

'They don't all have birthplaces like 'Oceanus',' Howard said with a laugh.

'Perhaps not, but they have a heritage that can't be bought or given away.'

The door was opened and the maid came in, giving Helen a close scrutiny as she came to the table. Tea was served, but before they could begin the door was opened again, and this time a tall, powerfully built man entered. He paused on the threshold when he saw Helen, then came forward slowly, his eyes staring intently at her.

'My other grandson, Fenton, son of my eldest son,' Edsel Ormond said. 'Meet Doctor Helen Farley, Fenton.'

'You're taking old Wyatt's place while

he's away!' Fenton Ormond remarked, coming around the table with one hand outstretched. 'Well that will be an improvement on the local medical services.' He took Helen's hand, completely covering it with his own, and she noticed the thick black hair growing on his wrist and the back of his hand. There were even bunches of the coarse stuff on his fingers between the knuckles and lower joints. His grip was firm, and he held Helen's gaze as he stood over her. 'I'm pleased to meet you, Doctor Farley. We're in the same line of business, you might say. You'll be taking care of the people around here, and I handle their animals.'

'In certain cases I expect you're hard put to tell which are the animals and which are the masters,' Edsel Ormond said, and there was grim amusement in his voice. 'Sit down, Fenton, and we'll commence. I've been kept waiting as it is.'

Fenton sat down at Helen's side, and she was instantly aware of his presence. There was a great deal of magnetism in his make-up. He was taller and bigger than Howard, but his features were not so attractive. He seemed larger and more coarse than his cousin, and at once Helen could sense the deepness of his mind. They began the meal, and while Edsel Ormond kept the general conversation going without trouble, Helen was aware that there was now a tension in the air that hadn't been apparent before Fenton's arrival.

After the meal Edsel was helped to his feet, and it was Howard who saw the old man out of the room. Fenton remained in his seat at Helen's side.

'Doctor, don't forget the arrangement we made this afternoon,' Edsel called from the doorway, 'I shall expect to see you in the very near future.'

'Very well, Mr Ormond,' she replied. 'I'll make it early in the next week.'

'Thank you. I shall be looking forward to your visit. Goodbye now.'

'Goodbye, and thank you for asking me here. I have thoroughly enjoyed every minute.'

Howard smiled at her as he helped his grandfather out, and when the door closed behind them Fenton turned to Helen.

'I'm sorry I was late in getting home,' he said without wasting any time. 'I suppose Howard has taken it upon himself to show you around. That was a pleasure I should have looked forward to. May I take you for a walk through the grounds this evening?'

'I don't know,' Helen replied slowly. She was taken aback by his abrupt manner. Their eyes met, and he held her glance with a bold stare.

'I suppose Howard has attended to that also,' he said. 'Never mind. Perhaps we can get together some evening when you've settled into our way of life. What does Grandfather want to see you about? Is he worried about his health?' He paused, then continued before Helen could reply. 'But that old man never worried about his health from the day he was born. He isn't the type. Has Howard shown you my dogs?'

'He didn't.'

'Then come with me if you've finished tea. I didn't expect to see you in the very near future.'

He got to his feet and waited for Helen to do the same, and there was a tight smile on his lips as he lead her towards the door, which opened as they reached it. Howard entered the room, and paused when he saw them.

'Going somewhere?' he asked Fenton.

'I'm showing the doctor my dogs,' the bigger man replied. 'You won't be coming, will you? Those animals know that you're scared of them, Howard.'

'Be very careful.' Howard spoke through his clenched teeth, and Helen saw that his face had paled a little. 'Those damned animals are dangerous. Don't open that gate while the doctor is there.'

'They wouldn't harm anyone!' The contempt in Fenton's tones was unmistakable.

'Well I think I'd better come along, just in case,' Howard said firmly, 'and I've a good mind to bring along a shotgun.'

'Rubbish. The dogs know that I'm their master, and you had better keep away. The sight of you only excites them. If you've made arrangements to take the doctor out this evening then don't worry about it. I'll bring her back into the house in one piece.'

'I'll see you later,' Howard said. 'Don't stand too close to the wire, will you?'

Helen nodded, not knowing what to say, aware that there was animosity between these two men, and she wondered at it. Was it caused by the estate that one of them would inherit? That seemed the likely source of trouble, but she was certain that Howard was not that much concerned about 'Oceanus'. She followed Fenton out of the house, and they walked along a path to the rear. As they turned the corner and came into view of a large wire enclosure there was a terrific outbreak of barking, and Helen saw several large dogs leaping and jumping against the wire in their separate pens. There were two Alsatians and a Great Dane. Other dogs, there were about a dozen in all, were hurling themselves at the wire, and they were making the most intense noise Helen had ever heard from animal throats.

'They look dangerous,' she ventured to remark as they crossed to the pens.

'Not they. I'm the master and they know it. They're hungry now. I feed them once a day, and this is feeding time. All animals are a bit intense at feeding time, as are some humans. You're not going to take a fancy to Howard, are you?'

'I beg your pardon!'

'That's all right. If you get to know me at all you'll soon find out that I jump from one subject to another and back again like a ping-pong ball. There's not much love lost between Howard and me. We're like a couple of dogs in a pen, with one bone between the two of us.'

'The bone being 'Oceanus',' Helen felt constrained to say.

'That's right. You're a perceptive girl.' He glanced at her and smiled thinly, and Helen saw that his dark eyes didn't show any emotion at all. They were like animal eyes, entirely bare of feeling. 'If you'll just stand very still here the dogs won't get too excited. They don't like strangers around. I won't be long feeding them.'

Helen nodded and halted, and she watched him feeding the dogs. There was a savagery in some of the animals that she found hard to believe. Were they deliberately enraged? Fenton Ormond seemed to be a strange man, deep and intense, and Howard and also Dr Wyatt had mentioned that Fenton was a cruel person. The dogs cowered when he approached them, and resumed their ferocious barking and snarling after he had passed them by. Only when he withdrew did they begin eating their food.

'Do you like animals?' Helen demanded as they walked away from the dogs.

'I'm a vet,' he replied, and laughed. 'Of course I like animals. I turn out at all hours of the night to attend them. It's like me asking you if you like people.'

They walked back to the house, and

when they reached a corner and stood out of view of the windows, Fenton Ormond reached out and touched Helen's arm. She looked at him quickly, her pulses racing, and he studied her face for a moment, a slow, almost sardonic smile on his face.

'I should like to see you one evening,' he said firmly. 'I expect you'd like a good guide to show you around the district, and I can sense that you're in love with Cornwall, aren't you?'

'That's right. My father steeped me in Cornwall's past, and I am a romantic.' She sighed. 'I don't know if that's a drawback or not!'

'That sort of thing never hurt anyone. I don't go for all that stuff myself. I used to read about it when I was a boy, but I soon grew out of that. Howard is the one for colourful history.'

Helen began to walk on, and he came up with her, walking very close.

'You haven't answered yes or no,' he prompted

'I don't know if I shall have any free

67

time to start with,' Helen said evasively. 'Perhaps we'd better wait and see.'

'Is that what you told Howard?'

'Do you think Howard has asked me out?' she countered with a smile.

'No doubt. He wouldn't waste any time with a person like you.'

'What about Julia Anslow?'

'You've met her?' He laughed loudly and shook his head. 'Julia is little more than a joke around here. She's waiting for Grandfather Edsel to die, and when she knows which of us will inherit 'Oceanus' she'll get serious. Howard has little time for her, and she doesn't appeal to me. I like my women to be soft underneath, but Julia is as hard as nails. If she were a better actress I might have paid more attention to her, but she's all right to take around socially.'

'Poor girl!' Helen shook her head. 'She's in for a rude awakening.'

'I've got no pity for her,' he said harshly.

'Then you are cruel.'

'Has Howard told you that?'

'That you're cruel?' Helen glanced at him. 'Are you?'

'I'm not like Howard, if that's what you mean. I'm strong and he's weak.'

'Yet he climbed that ledge along the cliffs when you dared him and you've never attempted it!'

'You have been getting a lot of local history.' Fenton paused again, and there was an intense light in his dark eyes as he regarded Helen. 'But you'll get the wrong picture if you rely too much on one source. Ask around and find out. I think it's the fairest way.'

'I'll do that. I'm fair in my approach to every subject.' Helen smiled.

'Then you'll come out with me one evening? I can show you some wonderful places along the coast. If you want your fill of smugglers and atmosphere then you won't find a better guide than Fenton Ormond.'

'I'll remember that, and call on you when I get some free time.' Helen spoke lightly, but she was aware of a curious sensation inside her. She felt attracted to Fenton Ormond, but not by any physical power of his. It was more like the hypnotic pull of a snake for a rabbit. She shivered as the comparison passed through her mind, and the sound of the barking dogs in the background sent icy shivers along her tingling spine.

'So Howard has got in first,' he commented. 'That's my bad luck. It's a pity that you chose a Friday to visit 'Oceanus'. But my turn will come, I promise you, Doctor Farley. You'll be seeing more of me.'

They entered the house, and Fenton saw her into the library, where Howard was seated by the window. There was a folded newspaper by Howard's arm, and he picked it up and tossed it aside when he turned around to see Helen approaching him. Fenton went out and closed the door loudly, and Howard got to his feet.

'Those damned dogs make an irritating din,' he complained. 'Don't tell me that you liked visiting them. They're more like wild beasts of prey than dogs, and I don't understand why Fenton keeps so many. Sometimes they whine and howl all through the night.'

Helen nodded. 'They seemed very ferocious to me,' she admitted. 'Do they get enough exercise, or are they in those pens all the time?'

'They get all their exercise at night,' Howard said. 'Fenton turns them loose before he goes to bed. They have the run of the grounds beyond the house. But don't worry if you ever have to come to Grandfather in the night. The dogs can't get around to the driveway.'

'They certainly don't like strangers,' Helen remarked.

'I'm not a stranger, but they'd tear me to pieces if they got the chance,' Howard said. 'But never mind about the dogs. Have you agreed to go out with Fenton?'

'How do you know that he's asked me?' Helen was aware that she had said the same thing to Fenton about Howard, and she was wondering what caused the animosity between them. They were of different temperaments, but that wasn't sufficient reason. Howard put up with Fenton because they were cousins, but Fenton was more intense, and she was certain that she had detected hatred in Fenton's tones when he had spoken of Howard. Was the large inheritance at the bottom of it? she wondered.

4

She spent an enjoyable evening in Howard's company. He proved a fascinating expert on local matters, and held her attention and imagination with his tales of smuggling. The library contained an extensive section on Cornwall, and Howard invited her to make free use of it any time she wished. When it was time for her to leave, Helen felt reluctant to go, but the shadows were closing in around the big house, and the sun was gone from the sky.

'I'd better start thinking about taking you home,' Howard said at length, and she could sense the same reluctance in him. 'I haven't enjoyed myself more on a Friday. I don't suppose I shall be lucky enough to see you every Friday, shall I?'

'I shall be working when Doctor

Wyatt goes away,' Helen replied. 'That's in ten days. But I shall be getting a day off, or at least part of a day. Doctor Wyatt has an arrangement, so he tells me, with a doctor who lives in the next village.'

'Tilby,' Howard said.

'That's right. When I want a night off Doctor Anderson will stand in for me, and I'll do the same for him. I don't know what night Doctor Wyatt has, but I dare say I can have Fridays.'

'Will you make that arrangement?' he asked anxiously. 'I don't get much time to myself as a rule, and when I am away from my business I'm usually alone. It will be a change to have someone like you to see and talk to.'

'Very well.' Helen nodded. 'I've enjoyed myself this evening. I think this house has cast a spell over me.'

'It has a lot of atmosphere, and it does enchant a romantic,' he agreed. 'You'll have to be very careful, Helen. When it is time for you to go back to London you'll find that you won't have the strength to make the decision. You'll be held here in Cornwall until you die.'

'My father said something like that. He always wanted to come back, but he never had the chance. I think I should like to settle down in these parts, if only out of respect for his memory. He has been in this very house!'

'I know how you feel,' Howard said, getting to his feet. 'You'll be welcome here at any time. You know that, don't you?'

'Thank you very much,' she replied.

They went out to the Bentley, and Howard stared up at the darkening sky. There was still a rosy hue to the west, but over the sea the sky was heavy with approaching night, and the sea was becoming remote and mysterious, the shadows stealing across it like jealous veils. Helen took a long shuddering breath and leaned back upon the rich upholstery. It had been a long day, and one of the most pleasant she could remember. Howard switched on the lights as he drove down to the gate, and darkness seemed to close in more quickly, as if trying to overpower the dazzling beams of the vehicle.

'You've made a great hit with Grandfather,' Howard said after they had negotiated the gates and were driving towards the village. 'I wonder why he wants to see you? He's been running on about you ever since Doctor Wyatt mentioned that he was going away from the practice for three months. But when he saw you this afternoon he changed his tune instantly. I hope that's a good omen, Helen. I don't want to see the old man die yet.'

'He's tough, so Doctor Wyatt tells me,' Helen replied. 'We'll do what we can to keep him going.'

'There is some tension building up in the house.' Howard's voice deepened as he spoke. 'I think Fenton is getting impatient about the estate. He did mention to Grandfather that whoever was going to inherit upon his death should be permitted to take control now, in order to save the place from going to ruin. There was a terrible row over it, and Doctor Wyatt had to come out to Grandfather. The least thing upsets the old man, and I do my best to keep him even-tempered.'

'Strong passions could be fatal for him,' Helen reminded. 'If he's suffering from cardiac asthma then he's got high blood pressure and heart trouble. At his age it wouldn't take a lot to push him over the edge.'

'I know, but when I've spoken to Fenton about toning down his ways, he just laughs and says that the old man will probably outlive the both of us.'

'I see. Well I'm coming to the house one afternoon during next week and, if I'm permitted, I shall thoroughly examine your grandfather. He's Doctor Wyatt's most important patient, and if I'm to treat him during the next three months I want to know for myself his exact condition.'

'We'll have another talk afterwards,' Howard said. He fell silent as they entered the village, and when he brought the car to a halt outside Doctor Wyatt's he switched out the headlights and leaned back in the seat. 'I'm so very glad that you decided to walk up by 'Oceanus' today,' he mused. 'I dread to think that you might have been here for three months without our meeting. But we're going to make the most of your stay here, and when you leave I hope you won't go too far away.'

'Doctor Wyatt needs a partner in his practice,' Helen said. 'He's going to engage one when he returns. I shall be given the opportunity, of course, but he wants to know if I shall be accepted by the local people. If I do all right in his absence then I expect to get the partnership.'

'Then let's start hoping that the people around here will take to you,' Howard said brightly. 'But Grandfather is the hardest man to please in these parts, and you've certainly won him over! I think the rest of it will be easy.'

Helen found herself hoping so as she prepared to leave the car. But he reached out a hand and grasped her arm.

'Don't go yet,' he begged. 'What about the weekend? I shall be free tomorrow evening and all day on Sunday. Don't let's waste any time. You'll be on your own and so shall I. After the way we've both enjoyed ourselves today it would be plain foolish to remain apart.' He paused, and Helen could feel a tugging inside her. He was a most attractive man, and during their few short hours together she had begun to take a liking to him.

'I don't suppose I shall be busy,' she said slowly.

'Good. Then may I call for you tomorrow evening? I'd like to take you for a drive. There are some very interesting caves just along the coast. We have some ourselves, that go right under the house, proof that in the old days some members of my family were actively engaged in smuggling. I'd love to show you around.'

'You've won me over,' Helen said. 'I'll

be expecting you tomorrow evening.'

'About seven.' His hands were on the steering wheel now, and he stared at her from his side of the car.

Helen could feel a tingling inside her. She had half expected him to kiss her, but he made no move in her direction, and she suppressed a sigh as she opened the door and alighted.

'I shan't be late,' he said. 'Seven sharp.'

'I'll be ready, Howard,' she replied, using his name for the first time, and he smiled happily. 'Goodnight, and thank you again for such an enchanting time.'

She stood for a moment after he had gone, and when the lights of the Bentley had vanished she glanced out to sea. There were lights out there on the smooth water, and she knew some of the fishermen were at work. The warm breeze that caressed her face was like the touch of a fairy hand, and as she turned reluctantly to enter the house she knew instinctively that whatever lay before her in the future, the past was as dead as if it had never been. There was only the future, bright and beckoning, before her, and for the first time since her father's death she felt a tiny spark of anticipation. She didn't feel alone any more!

Helen slept late next morning, and when she awoke the sun was shining in at the window. Getting out of bed, she went to the window, and narrowed her eyes against the glare of the sun. The sea was calm and the wind warm. It was to be another heavenly day, and Helen dressed slowly, trying to put her thoughts in order. She had a great collection of new impressions and sensations to store away, and a voice in her wondering mind was telling her firmly that an important phase of her life was beginning.

She went down to the kitchen to find Doctor Wyatt there, drinking coffee before setting out for his surgery, an office near the little fish market.

'I trust you enjoyed yourself yesterday,' he commented as the housekeeper poured coffee for Helen and began making toast for her breakfast.

'I had a wonderful time,' she replied with a laugh. 'I hope you're going to let me start working with you this morning.'

'You can come along to the surgery when you're ready, and I'll introduce you to some of the patients. I expect there will be some house calls to make, and you can drive me in your car, if you wish.'

'Wonderful. I feel such a fraud doing nothing while you're still hard at it, and you're the one who needs a holiday.'

'Nonsense, my girl. You're going to have a busy three months after I'm gone. Get all the rest you can before you start. I only hope you won't be run off your feet, that's all.'

'I'm sure I shan't be.' Helen smiled at him. She was very fond of her father's old friend. 'It will be summertime, and Father always said that Cornish people were very hardy.'

'They're good people, and once they

take to you there's no going back and no half-measures. But you're not like a stranger, Helen. Your father is of these parts.'

'Was,' Helen corrected with a little smile. She nodded. 'That's why I was so happy to come this way, Doctor Wyatt. I feel closer to the past, and I don't feel so lonely, knowing that Father has walked these roads and seen all these wonderful views before me.'

'I know how you must feel, my dear, and I can say without hesitation that I'm so very happy to have you here with me.' The old doctor got to his feet. 'Now you have a good breakfast and come along to the surgery when you're ready. I'll walk this morning. I feel like the exercise, but you can drive, and then we'll take care of the house calls together. It's not so much the addresses in the village itself that you need to familiarise yourself with. They're easy enough to find. But my practice covers a large part of the surrounding country, and on a dark night it isn't easy to find some of the by-roads and little clusters of cottages. But there's nothing to worry about. I have all next week to show you around.'

When he had left Helen began eating her breakfast, and she could not quell the tiny spark of excitement that brightened inside her. Her life seemed to have suddenly opened out after following a closed path for many years. But that was the way of it, and she was content now, knowing that she was performing a very useful job for the community, aware that outside influences could bring important pressures to bear upon her. When she thought of Howard Ormond a definite thrill passed through her, and she smiled slowly as she recalled their conversations. He was a most engaging man. There was no doubt about that. But so was Fenton Ormond, and the thrill turned to a shiver as coldness touched her heart. The cousins were not alike in appearance or manner, and where Howard exuded warmth and friendship, Fenton emitted troubling impulses that stirred her deeply and subconsciously.

She could not begin to understand Fenton Ormond.

Driving to the surgery a little later, Helen parked the car in the narrow back road and entered the building where Dr Wyatt had his office and surgery. The waiting-room contained several people, both men and women, waiting to see the doctor, and the receptionist, an old retired midwife who helped out the doctor, greeted her warmly.

'I'll tell Doctor you're here, Doctor Farley,' the old receptionist said. 'He's busy this morning, but there's nothing serious to handle. People are coming here every day with the same complaints. It isn't like your big London hospitals, is it? Won't you find this part of the country too quiet for your liking?'

'No. I'm going to enjoy every minute of my time here,' Helen replied.

The door opened at her back and she turned as a tall, broad-shouldered man entered. He paused to stare at her, and

Helen dropped her eyes to one of his hands, which he was holding up before him. She winced as she saw the big steel fish-hook that was embedded in the fleshy part of the hand, beneath the thumb. He grinned at her, noting her change of expression.

'Ned Pacey, what on earth have you been doing?' the receptionist cried. 'I brought him into the world, Doctor Farley, and he's been a constant source of trouble ever since.'

'It's nothing,' he commented, his eyes on Helen's face. He was fair-haired, and his blue eyes were sharp and bright. Despite the heat of the morning he was wearing a roll-neck fisherman's jersey, and his feet were encased in thick rubber thigh-boots turned down to below his knees. 'I'll need to have this cut out of me, and if the doctor will do it I shan't have to go into Radmin to the hospital.'

'Take him into the treatment-room, Doctor,' the receptionist ordered quickly. 'Don't let the other patients see that.

Some of them are quite ill enough as it is. I'll send Doctor Wyatt in.'

'Don't bother,' the fisherman replied, his eyes twinkling, and he showed no signs of pain, although the big hook must be hurting him greatly. 'You're the new doctor, aren't you?' His pale eyes held Helen's gaze. 'Well, let's see what you can do. Cut this out of me and make a neat job of it.'

Helen took a deep breath as she led him into the little treatment-room. Because the village was so far away from the hospital Doctor Wyatt performed many small operations himself, handling casualties in the area rather than subjecting the people to a five-mile drive to Radmin. The fisherman sat down, and Helen removed her white lace gloves, donned a white coat and washed her hands at the little sink. Doctor Wyatt came into the room as she turned to examine the wound.

'Hello, Doctor,' the fisherman greeted. 'It's nothing your new partner can't handle. I heard tell she had arrived, and

I wanted to get a look at her. She's even prettier than I was told. It was well worth getting hooked just to come along and see her.'

'That's enough of your flirting, Ned,' Doctor Wyatt said with a smile. 'I expect you took that hook deliberately, just to come here. But she's got Cornish blood in her, so don't try any of your tricks around her. Let me take a look at that hand, Helen. You'll be getting a lot of this sort of thing here, so I'd better explain the way we handle them. Ned wouldn't thank you to cut him open. He has to use that hand to work. Now.' He fell silent as he bent over the hand, and Helen watched him. She could see the steel point of the hook just under the skin. It had sunk deeply into the flesh before turning outward, and the man was well and truly hooked.

'It looks nasty,' she commented, glancing at the fisherman's grinning face.

'And it hurts,' he told her impishly, his blue eyes alight with devilment. 'If you weren't here now I'd be stretched out on the floor in a dead faint.'

'I wish you were,' Doctor Wyatt commented. 'Then you wouldn't feel it. Now stay quiet, Ned, and grit your teeth, man.' He glanced at Helen. 'Look,' he said. 'The point of the hook and the barb are near to the surface, so instead of cutting down to it we can continue to push it into the wound until the point and barb break surface. With the barb clear of the flesh we can cut it off, then work the rest of the hook backwards and out of the wound.'

'Don't talk about it,' Ned Pacey said. 'I can stand the pain, but I can't bear to listen to you.'

'All right, Ned.' Doctor Wyatt placed the man's hand on a rubber-sheeted table. 'If you're ready, then so am I. Do you want a local anaesthetic?'

'No. I can take it,' came the grim reply.

Helen watched as the doctor took hold of the hook between finger and thumb, and she frowned as he suddenly exerted his strength and forced the hook deeper into the flesh, using a semi-circular motion to bring the point and barb to the surface. The flesh was pierced and the barb appeared. Ned Pacey grunted and leaned back in the chair, but he grinned at Helen.

'That's the worst part of it, Ned,' Doctor Wyatt said. 'Shan't be a moment now.' He took up a pair of silver cutters and snipped off the point and the barb from the hook. 'Now to take it back again,' he commented, and worked the rest of the hook out of the wound 'There you are, Ned, it's out. You'd better be more careful in future. A man of your experience shouldn't be getting caught like that, you know.'

'I'm breaking in Tolliver's youngster to the game,' the fisherman explained, and watched Helen's face as he spoke. 'He fouled the troll lines accidentally, and this was the result.'

'Perhaps you'll put a dressing on the wound,' Doctor Wyatt said to Helen. 'I left old Mrs Hagen in the consulting-room, and if I don't get back to her and send her on her way we'll get behind for the rest of the day.'

He left Helen to it, and she cleansed the wound and bandaged the hand.

'That's fixed it,' she said as she snipped off the ends of the knot she had tied. 'Don't work it too hard today, will you? Perhaps you'd better let us look at it on Monday.'

'I'll call in without fail,' the man replied, getting to his feet. He towered over her, his pale eyes bright and sharp, his hair long down his neck and curling over his collar. 'I wouldn't mind being ill with you to come and see me, Doctor. I wonder what a man has to do to get you to see him when you're off duty!'

'A man wanting to see me off duty usually asks me,' Helen replied with a smile.

'I hadn't thought it would be so simple,' he retorted, showing strong white teeth and bending slightly towards her. 'I should like to see you off-duty, Doctor Farley. Would it be possible?'

'Not this week or next,' she replied

gently. 'Perhaps some other time.'

'I'll not wait to get a hook into me before dropping in here to see you,' he warned. 'I'll wait until the old doctor has gone and you're settled into your routine. Goodbye for now.'

'Goodbye, Mr Pacey,' Helen replied.

She shook her head slowly as he departed, and then she cleaned the instruments used and restored the room to its former state. She kept on the white coat as she went along the passage to the consulting-room, and tapping at the door she entered to find Dr Wyatt talking to an old lady.

Helen found that the local people were friendly, despite what she had heard to the contrary. The men, as they came into the room, seemed a little embarrassed to start with, but Helen talked to them, and Dr Wyatt was content to let her take the rest of his surgery. The women were immediately at ease with Helen, and by the time the last patient had gone Dr Wyatt was smiling happily.

'I can see that there will be no problems while I'm away,' he remarked. 'You're going to get on famously, Helen, and that gives me a clear mind. I don't mind admitting that I was worried about going, but seeing you in action has more than reassured me. I think you'd better think about taking up a partnership with me while I'm away, and have your answer ready when I get back.'

'Don't act impulsively,' Helen replied with a smile. 'I'm beginning to think that it was you who needed confidence in me and not the patients.'

'Perhaps you've hit the nail on the head,' he retorted. There was a gleam in his bright blue eyes. 'Anyway, I'm convinced now, so consider my offer of a partnership, will you?'

'I'll think very seriously about it,' Helen told him. 'I have to make a decision about my future. I was at the crossroads when I accepted your offer to come here, and these next three months will give me a breathing space in which to think.'

'It may turn out a lot easier than you think,' the old doctor said with a twinkle in his eyes. 'You could get interested in one of the local men, you know. I've never known Howard Ormond to take an interest in any girl, but he was keen to see you yesterday. I watched him from the window when you came home yesterday afternoon to change. You could do a lot worse than Howard, Helen. He's rich in his own right, apart from what he might get from Edsel's estate when the old man goes. Have you met Fenton yet?'

'He came in while we were having tea,' Helen said, and her mind went back to the previous afternoon. 'I don't know what to make of him, Doctor. He seems to be a mixture of this and that.'

'I wouldn't advise you to get too friendly with him!'

'Why not? Is there some mystery surrounding him, some shadow over his life?'

'Is that the impression you've gained?' the doctor countered.

'I didn't get a clear impression because Howard talked about him before we met. But I didn't like the impressions I picked up during the evening. He's got a powerful magnetism that doesn't attract or repel. It's something between the two. I found him fascinating, to tell you the truth, but not in the way a woman would find a man attractive. While I was near him I got some instinctive warnings from my intuition. I don't think I want to get to know him as a friend.'

'I know exactly what you mean,' Doctor Wyatt said. 'I don't know of anything that can be held against Fenton Ormond, but there is talk about him in these parts. Of course there is talk about the whole family, but that is to be expected when Edsel lives in a place like 'Oceanus', and they are filthy rich. But Howard is a nice chap, and you could do much worse.'

'He's not at all worried about the estate, but it seems that Fenton is,' Helen remarked. 'There could be trouble between those two when the old man dies.'

'I've thought that all along, and I

don't know why Howard persists in living at 'Oceanus'. His father's business is doing very well, and he could well afford to buy himself a house near the factory. I suppose he has a love for the estate. He's lived there most of his life, and no doubt he acts as a buffer between Fenton and the old man.' Doctor Wyatt sighed and shook his head. 'But let's make a start with the house calls, shall we? There aren't all that many this morning. They're a healthy lot around here, and usually at this time of the year I have only the very old and the chronic sick to see. The list hardly varies from one day to another, I can tell you. Sometimes I feel that I'd give a pension just to have some rare disease crop up, or an epidemic of some sort.'

'Doctor!' Helen said in mock severe tones. 'The next step to that kind of thinking is poisoning the town's water supply or putting the wrong medicine into the patients' prescriptions.'

'That's an idea,' he replied with a

laugh, and they left the room and prepared to visit the sick patients in their homes.

Helen enjoyed the morning's work, for Doctor Wyatt accompanied her in a supervisory capacity, just directing her to the homes of the patients and introducing her. He watched her handling of the patients, and at lunch-time, as they were driving back to the house, he told her what he thought of her skill.

'You certainly know how to handle them,' he said with a smile. 'Some of them responded better to you than they've ever done to me. Perhaps they won't want me back when I return.'

'There's not much fear of that!' Helen replied with a laugh. 'They all think quite highly of you.'

'But we haven't visited Edsel Ormond together,' he said. 'I know you were there yesterday, and that's something. But treating Edsel is another matter.'

'But I didn't tell you,' Helen said, and explained how Edsel had given orders for the windows in the house to be opened for two hours each day. She smiled at the expression which crossed the doctor's face as he stared at her. 'And he's asked me to call on him one afternoon during next week.'

'Well, that's really the limit!' Dr Wyatt shook his head slowly. 'For years I've been trying to convince him that I know best about his health, and he's never taken the slightest notice of me. Now you come along, and in one afternoon you've got him under your thumb. We must follow up this advantage, Helen. But I wonder why he wants to see you! Something is in the mind. Don't let him catch you out for anything. He's a strange man, and I shouldn't be at all surprised if he was a little insane. He certainly acts like it at times.'

'I don't think so,' Helen replied slowly. 'He struck me as being an extremely wise person. He might put on an act at times, but it is only an act. There's nothing wrong with the balance of his mind.'

'I wish I could be as firm in an opinion on Fenton Ormond,' the doctor said, and Helen could not but agree.

The conversation ended when they arrived at the house, but Helen could not help thinking about 'Oceanus' and its occupants. Howard she could understand, and she liked him. Edsel was an old man, and entitled to respect and understanding, but Fenton was strange, despite his exterior. There were deep currents of emotion in him, she was certain, and she could not rid herself of the thought that in the future she might find out more about him, and it was strange that she felt reluctant to want to do so.

5

As the time for Howard's arrival neared, Helen felt a growing anticipation, and she was ready long before she expected to see the big Bentley pulling up outside the gate. She stayed in her room overlooking the sea and watched the road for the first sign of the car, and when it turned into view she rushed to her mirror for a last glance at her reflection before hurrying down the stairs and out to the gate. She reached the narrow pavement outside the house as Howard brought the car to a standstill.

'Hello,' he greeted, opening the door and alighting. 'I must say you surprise me. I thought I might have to wait several minutes.'

'My medical training,' Helen replied as he escorted her around the car and opened the door for her. 'The first rule is punctuality.' She got into the car and he closed the door on her. Helen watched his tall figure as he went back around the car.

'Where would you like to go?' he asked as he seated himself beside her. 'Have you heard of any exciting places that you feel you must visit?'

'I've heard of so many! But I'll leave it to you. I'm sure your tastes are about the same as mine.'

He smiled as he started the car, and when he had turned round he drove quickly out of the village. Helen took a deep breath as she relaxed. It seemed now that she had waited a long time for this evening, and it startled her to realise that she had been looking forward to being in his company again. Glancing at his profile as they went on, Helen found herself being attracted to him. She wondered at it, knowing with cold certainty that since Gary Milton had treated her badly she had lost all interest in men.

'It's a beautiful evening,' he said at

length, glancing at her. 'Shall we take a run down to St Ann's? There's a yacht basin there, and I belong to the club. Do you like sailing, or have you never been?'

'I've never been,' Helen replied. 'But I should imagine it's a wonderful sensation.'

'Are you a good sailor?' he demanded.

'I've been across a ferry or two, and along the Thames,' she said with a smile. 'But that isn't the same thing, is it?'

'Not exactly, but there's nothing to worry about. We'll soon find out if you do have a flair for it. If you do, then we can spend some very nice times together.'

'I'm only here for three months,' Helen reminded him, and he looked sideways at her and smiled.

'Perhaps,' he retorted, and despite her tight grip upon her emotions, Helen felt a spurt of interest at his words.

The evening was warm and clear, and there were no clouds in the perfectly blue sky. The windows of the car were wound down and the breeze that came in around Helen's head was cooled by the speed of the car. She listened to the sound of the tyres swishing along the road, and was soothed by the noise. The sun was still brilliant, and she narrowed her eyes and lifted a hand to her forehead against the glare.

'Wait until the summer really starts,' he said, after a long silence. 'This is a cold day by comparison. I hope you won't be too busy while Doctor Wyatt is away. I'm hoping to see something of you in your free time.' He paused, and then changed the subject. 'Edsel was speaking about you today,' he went on. 'You've certainly made a conquest there. He's looking forward to seeing you one afternoon during the week.'

'I'll make it on Monday, if he's getting impatient,' Helen suggested. 'Have you any idea what he wants? Is it about his health?'

'I don't know. The old man can be very close-mouthed when he likes. If he wants me to know, then he'll tell me.'

Howard fell silent again, and Helen felt quite comfortable in his company. The silence didn't turn awkward, and they remained so until the car turned a bend in the road and Helen saw before them the fishing village of St Ann's.

The road wound down the cliffs to the low promenade, where the small cottages and houses were huddled together as if in fear of the sea only yards away. Howard drove along until they reached the small harbour, and then he parked the car on a wide stretch of coarse grass and they got out of the vehicle.

'This way,' he said as he locked the doors. He led Helen along a path and they climbed a great pile of shingle that looked as if it were part of the sea-defences. Pausing on the top, Howard waited for Helen to take a look at the view before them. Helen gasped in pleasure, taken completely by surprise.

The land on the other side of the shingle was low and marshy, and there were great sheets of open water in the distance, all sparkling like carpets of quicksilver in the lowering sun. To the left was a huddle of buildings, and many little landing stages jutting out into the bright water. But what took Helen's eyes were the great number of yachts of all models and classes, some with white sails, others with red or blue, and they were sailing and tacking about like so many strange water creatures in search of food. There was the sound of powerful outboard motors in the distance, and Howard pointed away to the right, where speedboats were pulling along water-skiers.

'This is a very busy place during the hot months, Helen,' Howard said. 'Can you swim?'

'Yes, although I haven't done so for a few years now. But I was something of a schoolgirl champion in the old days.'

'We have a private beach below the house,' he went on. 'I don't like crowds, and if you'd like to swim again, then why don't you come along tomorrow for the day?'

'I don't have a bathing suit, and this is Saturday evening,' she reminded. 'But I'd love to sun-bathe.'

'Then, I'll pick you up in the morning about ten-thirty,' he said with satisfaction. 'We'll have a picnic on the beach, if you like, or we could go up to the house for lunch. But that is all by the way. I was wondering what to do with myself tomorrow, and meeting you has solved that problem. What do you say?'

'It's a wonderful idea,' Helen told him.

'Good. Ten-thirty, then. Now let's go along to the club-house and have a drink. We shan't bother to go out this evening. It is getting a bit late now, don't you think?'

'I expect so.' Helen couldn't take her eyes off the tiny boats out there on the smooth water.

'I've got a motor cruiser down there, too,' Howard said. 'I don't use it very often now, and that's a pity, but with you to show around I might work up some of the old passions again. I'd like to show you a good time while you're here, Helen.'

'Thank you, you're very kind,' she replied as they walked along the top of the shingle bar and then followed a footpath down to the narrow dirt road that led among the cluster of buildings and boatsheds at the water's edge. 'I've seen places like this in films, and I've always yearned to try some of these activities.'

'Then you shall. If you go back to London in three months, then you'll take a great many new experiences with you. In fact, you may enjoy yourself so very much that you won't want to return.'

'And that's quite possible,' Helen retorted.

'We'll see.' Howard walked easily at her side as they approached the club-house, and he waved and spoke to several men as they passed. 'They're a jolly crowd here, Helen, and I think you'll like them. Once they get to know you they'll see that you have a good time. But I hope too many of my friends won't ask you out or I shan't see you at all until you come up to 'Oceanus' after three months to say goodbye.'

'I'm not one for the mad whirl,' she said gently. 'I do expect to be rather busy during the next three months, and what little free time I get will be spent in and around Tredporth.'

'That's what I like to hear.' He took her elbow as they mounted the steps to the club-house, and upon entering Helen looked around to find herself in the large bar. 'What about a drink?' he demanded. 'I don't make much of a habit of it myself, but I like to be social. It's a hot evening and it's been a very long sunny day.'

'A port and lemon, please,' Helen said as he ushered her to a seat, and he nodded and smiled as he walked to the bar.

Helen looked around with interest, and enjoyed the atmosphere of the little place. There were yachting trophies on the walls, and many pictures of all kinds of sailing craft. Most of the men present were wearing white, peaked yachting caps, and the women were in summery dresses or jeans and blouses.

Howard returned with their drinks, and he sighed as he sat down. He kept glancing around, nodding at acquaintances, and when he caught Helen's eye he smiled.

'There are a lot of curious people around here this evening,' he commented. 'I'm rarely seen in the company of a woman, and never one as lovely as you.'

'Thank you for the compliment,' Helen said to cover her warmth. The tone in his voice made her tremble. 'Don't you like lovely women, or haven't you had time to take them out?'

'It isn't a case of one or the other,' he retorted with a smile. 'I've just never had the chance, I suppose. I'm not saying there are no lovely women in these parts, but I've yet to meet one who really interested me — present company excepted, of course. But there will be some wagging tongues over the weekend, and no doubt you'll make an enemy or two.'

'That sounds ridiculous,' Helen retorted. 'I'm not the type to make enemies.'

'There are several eligible women in the locality who have their eyes on me,' Howard said seriously, although his eyes were gleaming as he stared at her. 'Or rather, I should say they have their eyes on 'Oceanus'. You've met Julia Anslow. She's on for certain, and the prize must be very big because she and the others are never disappointed by set-backs.'

'Such as?' Helen prompted.

'Such as you coming along and stepping straight into the picture. I don't really know what to make of the situation as it stands.' He broke off and stared across the room. 'Damn! There's Fenton. I didn't know he was coming in here this evening. I hope he's not coming over.'

Helen looked around, and saw Fenton Ormond standing in a doorway on the far side of the bar. He was bareheaded, standing over the two young men in his company. She saw that he had spotted them right away, and he said something to his companions, then left them and walked lazily towards the table where Helen and Howard sat. He smiled tightly as he came up, and again Helen got the feeling that there was more to him than showed in his manner.

'Hello,' he greeted carelessly. 'I didn't know you were coming here this evening or I would have put on my best suit. What do you think of our little club, Helen?'

'I like it,' she replied easily, noting his use of her name.

'I suppose Howard has asked you to go sailing and swimming with him,' Fenton went on, ignoring his cousin, and Helen, glancing at Howard, was surprised to see his face showing signs of tension, even anger, as he waited for Fenton to go.

'He has, and I've agreed,' Helen said, stifling the pang of worry that shot through her.

'What about fishing, then? He's not so keen on that, and I like it. Don't tell me that you wouldn't like to go out in a boat and catch some very large fish. I won't take a refusal. I insist that you accompany me. I'm free tomorrow, so what about you?'

'I'm sorry, but I have an engagement for tomorrow.'

'All day tomorrow,' Howard put in, his face now expressionless. He smiled at Helen as she glanced at him, but his ease of manner had deserted him.

'Well, I'm a very busy man during the week, not like an ordinary business-man,' Fenton said with a smile. 'You're a doctor and you should understand. So I'm putting forward an offer for the following weekend. Don't say you won't come because I shan't accept a refusal.'

'I'm afraid next Sunday is Doctor Wyatt's last day,' Helen apologised. 'I daren't make any arrangements without first consulting him. I am sorry.'

'And so am I!' Fenton stared at her

for a moment, and she moved uncomfortably under the power of his gaze. 'So Fate is conspiring against me! Well, I can fight against Fate. I'm no stranger to that sort of thing. However I'll leave you to Howard's tender mercies this evening. I have no wish to intrude. I'll call you during the week, and remember that I asked first about next Sunday.'

He smiled and turned away, and Howard stirred himself as if awakening from a spell. He sighed as he watched Fenton cross to the bar.

'He's a very attractive man!' Helen said, wanting to get Howard to talk about his cousin, hoping to learn something about the both of them.

'And he knows it,' Howard replied, and left it at that.

Within a few minutes Helen was aware that the evening for Howard had been spoiled, and as she finished her drink she glanced at him.

'Would you like to be going?' she asked.

'I suppose we could go for a walk,' he

replied almost curtly, and drained his glass and got to his feet without further ado. He came around the table to help Helen to her feet, and she noticed that he kept his eyes off Fenton Ormond as they walked to the door. But Helen glanced towards the bar, saw that Fenton was watching her, and dropped her gaze as he smiled and waved farewell. She looked at him again immediately and smiled, not wanting him to get any impression that she disapproved of him, but he had already turned back to the company of the men with him, and she regarded his broad back as a sigh gusted through her.

Outside, the night was closing in. The sun was down and there was very little gold in the heavens to mark its passing. The breeze had turned surprisingly cold, and Helen suppressed a shiver as they walked to the shingle slope and ascended it.

'Cold?' Howard demanded. 'These evenings are deceptive, aren't they?' He was back to normal now, and Helen refused to let her thoughts dwell upon the subject.

'It's quite a change from the day,' she replied. 'I should have had more sense and brought along a cardigan.'

'We'll go for a drive instead of a walk,' he said, and unlocked the car. He was silent while he turned the vehicle, and when he was driving back out of the village he cast a quick glance at Helen. 'I'm sorry about that back there,' he said. 'It's no use trying to keep it from you. You're the family doctor, whether you like it or not. I don't get along with Fenton because he doesn't choose to be friends. He's too concerned about the estate and who is going to get it. When we're alone at the house he cuts me dead, but you see how he acts when other people are around. You would think he and I are the best of friends. Well, I can't blow hot and cold like that. I'm not such a good actor, and I'm not all that concerned about 'Oceanus'. I like the place because my father was born and brought up there. I'd like to inherit it, because I'm sure Fenton would very soon ruin it and all it stands for if he got his hands upon it.' He sighed. 'I shouldn't go on like this, I know, but I don't want you getting the wrong impressions, Helen.'

'I think I do understand,' she said gently. 'I hope you get what you want. But surely your grandfather knows both you and Fenton very well. I'm sure he has the estate at heart, and he wouldn't do anything to cause trouble.'

'Grandfather is past it now. I don't think he cares what happens after he's gone. He's often said that he'd like to see a tidal wave come up from the sea and sweep the house and everything in it out of existence.'

'I'm sure he doesn't mean that. There was pride in him when he spoke about 'Oceanus'.'

'That's the point. He's passionately in love with the place, but he has the idea that Fenton and I are not suited to taking care of it.'

'You're both pretty successful men in the world,' Helen pointed out.

'That counts for nothing with Grandfather,' he replied morosely. They were silent for some time, and then he made an effort to break out of the mood that seemed to have taken hold of him. 'You must think that we are a strange family,' he commented, 'but Fenton always makes me like that when he gets socially minded. He's not the type, really, and only comes out of his shell when there's something in sight that he wants. He is beginning to show an interest in you, Helen, and I don't like it. The worst mistake you could make would be to fall for Fenton's charm.'

'I have no intention of falling for anyone,' she retorted firmly.

'You're a romantic, and with this kind of setting you're easy prey for a man like Fenton.'

'I don't see anything wrong with him,' Helen countered. 'He's strange, I'll grant you that, but he's handsome, attractive, and as Julia Anslow would point out, no doubt, he has great expectations.'

'But that's not the way you think,' he protested sternly. He looked at her, trying to pick out her expression in the gathering gloom, and she smiled to show that she was just joking. He laughed and shrugged. 'All right, so I'm getting a bit too intense. I'm sorry. Let's forget about Fenton, shall we? It's what he wants. He'd have a good laugh if he knew I was upset about our meeting him this evening.'

The big car roared on through the evening, and Helen tried to relax, but there were certain thoughts in her mind that gave her no rest. Had she made a mistake in becoming involved with the Ormond family? She had taken it for granted from Doctor Wyatt's words that Edsel Ormond was the most important patient in the practice, not that he would receive better treatment than anyone else, and she had acted accordingly upon meeting Howard the previous afternoon. But she did not want to get mixed up in their personal lives. The situation was fraught with complication, and she had a sudden premonition that a climax was fast approaching the Ormonds. If she got to know them too well she might become caught up in their petty hates and jealousies, and that would never do. She warned herself to be careful, and with that decision made she felt a little awkward at Howard's side.

He was very nice, she told herself, studying his dark profile as he sent the Bentley on and on. He seemed her type, and she knew she could accept him as a friend without trouble or second thought. But that wouldn't suit Fenton Ormond. She suppressed a shiver as she thought of him, with his handsome face and intense brown eyes. He had made it obvious from the very first moment of their meeting that he was interested in her, and now Helen was wondering if his interest stemmed from his desire to take her away from Howard. She shook her head slowly as she considered it, and decided that appearances were deceptive. On the face of it she had walked into a pleasant situation, where Howard was interested enough to see her and show her a good time, but there seemed to be dark pangs in her mind, warning, irritating with their unpleasant aspects. What could come that troubled her subconscious mind, her intuition? She did not know, but she knew she had to be prepared for anything.

For the rest of that evening she felt that she was sitting on the edge of a cliff, and when Howard turned for home she began to wonder what was in his mind. Had he become attracted to her? Would he try and kiss her this evening? She smiled a little, unable to prevent her womanly feelings from asserting themselves. She would like to be kissed by him! The knowledge did not surprise her, but she was disappointed, for when they reached the village he dropped her off with a gentle goodnight and a reminder that he would pick her up at ten-thirty next morning.

Helen went in to bed with her emotions ruffled, her desires unsatisfied. But she consoled herself with the thought that there was always tomorrow!

6

Sunday turned out to be a heavenly day. Helen was ready, filled with excitement like a schoolgirl, long before the appointed hour, and when Howard arrived she took her leave of a smiling Doctor Wyatt and hurried out to the car. Getting in beside Howard, she studied him closely, wondering if his mood had changed from the previous evening, and he was smiling light-heartedly.

'I'm so glad the weather is bright,' he said. 'Are you still set upon trying our private beach?'

'I can think of nothing better today,' Helen replied.

'Good. Lucy, our maid, has a new bathing suit that she hasn't tried yet. I took the liberty of asking her at breakfast if she had anything suitable for you. She's going to let you try it, and if it fits then you can have it and she'll buy another. She wouldn't use it today, anyway.'

'That sounds wonderful,' Helen told him, and he smiled as he turned the car and drove out of the village.

The gates were open when they reached 'Oceanus', and Howard didn't bother to get out and close them. He drove around to the rear of the house and left the big car in front of the garage. Helen looked around for signs of Fenton as they walked towards the house, but there was no sign of him. The dogs were yelping and barking, leaping against the high wire that held them captive, and Helen suppressed a tremor as she imagined one of them escaping. They were such vicious dogs.

'Lucy will have taken the things we'll need down to the beach,' Howard said. 'But come into the house to try on that swimsuit. It's a two-piece, and you're about Lucy's size, so there shouldn't be any trouble there. I'm not a very good swimmer myself, but I manage fairly well. I don't have a lot of confidence in the water, that's the trouble. I always get alarmed when only my head is out of the water and I can't feel the bottom with my feet.'

Helen smiled and they entered the house.

'How is your grandfather this morning?' she asked.

'I wouldn't know. No one bothers him until he rings for attention. He's in his room, and at about eleven he'll ring for the Sunday papers. He doesn't eat any breakfast, and only a light lunch. I wouldn't dare disturb him or attempt to break his routine. I don't think he's happy unless someone tries to upset him. I don't know why he's cultivated such a grouchy manner. He never used to be like that.'

'It must be his age,' Helen suggested, 'and of course his complaint will have a lot to do with it.'

'If you'll just wait here I'll fetch Lucy and she'll give you the swimsuit,' he said, moving away, and Helen moved slowly along the hall, looking at some of the paintings hung on the dark panelled walls. She found herself feeling tense, filled with anticipation, and she knew it was because she was afraid that Fenton would suddenly appear before her.

Howard returned with the maid, who handed Helen a bikini of yellow satin trimmed with black lace.

'Thank you so much, Lucy,' Helen said. 'It's very kind of you.'

'That's all right, Doctor,' the maid replied. 'I didn't like the colours after I'd bought it. They'll suit you better than me.'

'You must get yourself another one and let me have the bill,' Helen told the girl. 'May I try this on now?'

'Take her up to the spare bedroom,' Howard directed. 'Have you taken everything down to the beach that we may need, Lucy?'

The girl nodded as she took Helen up the stairs, and in the bedroom Helen tried on the bikini, finding that it was a perfect fit. She kept it on and pulled on her skirt and blouse over it. Leaving the room, she thanked the waiting Lucy again, who seemed quite pleased that the swimsuit fitted.

'I hope you'll have a nice time today, Doctor,' the girl said warmly as they descended the stairs. They found Howard waiting for them, and he was eager to know if the bikini fitted.

'Good,' he said when Helen told him that it did. 'Let's waste no further time. Are we coming back to the house for lunch, Lucy.'

'Whatever you please,' the girl replied. 'I can bring a basket down with a cold lunch, if you wish.'

'I think we'll settle for that,' he said slowly, and Helen guessed that he was thinking about Fenton. She had the feeling herself that she didn't want to see his cousin. Apart from the fact that Fenton's presence had some adverse effect upon Howard, Helen was reluctant to give Fenton any chance of becoming friendly. Her intuition was still at work inside her.

They left the house and walked along a paved path to the cliffs. At a spot where the ground dipped steeply the height of the cliffs above the sea was halved, and Helen saw a flight of wooden steps fixed to the cliff-face. There were handrails, and wooden landings had been fixed at twenty-foot intervals. Howard went first, glancing back to see if she was nervous, but Helen felt exhilarated, and she smiled at him.

On the narrow strip of bright yellow sand that lay hemmed in by sea and cliffs, there was a small round table with a striped umbrella rising up out of its centre. On the table lay several large towels, and Howard's bathing trunks. He paused and Helen halted at his side. They both glanced around, and the peacefulness in the little cove seemed to close in around them like a cloak. The sky was perfect, cloudless and deep blue in colour, and the sea showed barely a ripple on its broad expanse. Even the waves that lapped the beach were small and gentle.

'I'll go over there behind those rocks to change,' Howard said, taking up his blue trunks. 'The water should be warm this morning.'

Helen watched him as he walked across the sand. She could tell by the marks on the hard-packed sand that at high tide the water reached far above the beach. She imagined standing on the wooden steps above high water when there was a strong wind blowing, and in her imagination she could see the white-topped waves thundering in to attack the cliffs in their eternal battles, the white spray flying in the wind and the anger of the elements unleashed with all Nature's fury.

But today there was no hint of anger anywhere, and she took off her blouse and stepped out of her skirt, excitement racing through her at the caress of the warm breeze against her skin. Howard was coming back, looking big and strong in his trunks. He smiled as he tossed his clothes on the table.

'Race you?' he demanded, and Helen nodded eagerly and ran towards the water without more ado. Her fast movement took him by surprise, and she left him standing, but he soon caught up with her, but made no attempt to pass her.

The water was a hundred yards away, and they reached it together, splashing through the shallows until they could run no further. Helen launched herself forward in a flat dive, and went under the surface, immediately lost in another world, and she closed her eyes at the pleasure of the water. She felt a hand touch her cheek, and opened her eyes to see the dim figure of Howard moving along at her side, and they broke surface together, treading water, blowing and gasping, and Helen was laughing.

'This is glorious,' she spluttered, her eyes intent upon his face. 'What a wonderful place you have here.'

'It's lonely on one's own,' he retorted with a wry smile. 'Perhaps I can induce you to spend all your Sundays here with me, when you're able.'

'You're tempting me greatly,' Helen replied, starting to swim away from him with steady, powerful strokes. 'Is it at all dangerous bathing here?'

'Sometimes, when the tide is going out,' he replied, keeping at her side. 'It's safe enough along the shore, but farther out there's a circular current that reaches into the cove from the open sea, and if you get into its clutches you'll have a job to get back to the beach. But the tide is coming in now, and we've got several hours before we have to watch out.'

He proved to be a better swimmer than he had admitted, and Helen paced him, striking out strongly. It had been some years since she was last in the water, but she found to her surprise that it might have been only days ago when she had competed in the swimming competitions of her schooldays.

They swam for almost an hour, splashing each other and diving, enjoying themselves with the careless abandonment of children. They were far out from the beach, and Helen was beginning to feel the invisible strength of a current, but it was pushing her towards the shore, trying to carry her to a point where the tiny strip of sand terminated in high cliffs at the edge of the cove. She was several yards from Howard, who was striking around powerfully, thoroughly enjoying himself, when a dark object suddenly arose from the depths and broke surface between them. She blinked in surprise, for it was a man's head, and the next instant she found herself staring into Fenton's grinning face.

'Hello there,' he greeted, swimming close, ignoring Howard, who was gazing in shock at them. 'I saw you from the cliff top, and you looked so happy in here that I just had to come and join you. You're a good swimmer, Helen, but Howard is letting you get a bit too far out. Can you feel the current? Once you get out of the cove it won't let go of you. It takes a really strong swimmer to battle against it. Come this way. There's something I want to show you.'

'We'd better get back to shore now, Helen,' Howard called. 'We've been in here for a long time. You ought to take it easy. This is the first time, you know.'

'I want to show her Perrin's Cave,' Fenton said, keeping between Helen and Howard.

'She won't want to dive down into that place,' Howard objected. 'Are you crazy, Fenton?'

'Not crazy, just unafraid,' Fenton replied with a grin. 'Come on, Helen, and you'll see something that will enchant you for the rest of your life.'

Helen was intrigued by his words, but Howard came striking desperately to her side, glaring at Fenton before showing Helen his worried face.

'Helen, you're not to go,' he said quickly, blowing water as he stayed at her side. 'I brought you here today and I feel responsible for you. It's dangerous to dive into that cave. I did it once and almost drowned.'

'Only because you panicked,' Fenton

said, treading water and grinning. 'I can take care of Helen. Don't try to bar her from pleasure just because you're afraid, Howard. She isn't the type to get frightened.'

'What is Perrin's Cave?' Helen demanded, striking slowly for the distant shore, knowing that they would follow her. She didn't want an argument taking place some three hundred yards out in the bay.

'It's got an underwater entrance, about twenty feet down,' Howard spluttered, swimming at her side. 'The cave itself is beautiful, like a great fairy hall, with glistening stones like jewels set in the walls and roof. Fenton took down a lantern one time, and I was fool enough to dive down, although I must say the beauty down there was well worth the risk of diving down to see it. The trouble is, the entrance is only large enough to permit one person at a time to travel along it. You have to dive about twenty feet, find the entrance, then swim ten yards along the narrow tunnel until you get inside the cave. If you lost your nerve half-way you'd probably drown.'

'It sounds intriguing,' Helen ventured.

'It's something you must see before you leave Cornwall,' Fenton said, swimming strongly to come up on Helen's other side. 'There's no danger really to a strong swimmer who's got a good nerve. There's a sandy floor to the back of the cave, and signs that smugglers used it once, long ago.'

'That sounds even better,' Helen remarked, turning an interested face towards Howard. 'I won't attempt it if you really think it's dangerous, but if you've been in there and come out then it should be all right.'

'Not this morning,' Howard said firmly. 'Wait until the tide starts going out. At low tide there's about twenty feet of water over that entrance. Right now there's a lot more. If you are really keen, Helen, I'll go down with you this afternoon.'

'You'll never make it, Howard,' Fenton said, and there was a jeering note in his voice that jangled against Helen's nerves. 'Do you remember the last time you were down there? Or I should say the first and last time? You never went there again, did you?' He laughed harshly. They were nearing the shore now. 'I'll tell you about it, Helen. I told Howard what it was like — we were barely youths then — and he decided to have a look. He lost his nerve half-way along the tunnel, and if I hadn't been close behind him he would have drowned. I got him into the cave, and there he wanted to stay. Nothing would induce him to make the return dive. In the end I had to fetch a rope and tie him. I dragged him out.' He laughed again. 'After that, do you think you'll ever have the nerve to go back, Howard?'

'I was only a youngster when that happened,' Howard said thinly. He stood up suddenly, and at the same moment Helen's feet found the bottom.

135

'It was you who scared me at the time, I recall, and not the dive or the tunnel. Anyway, we have some skin diving equipment up at the house. We can do it in style now, if we want to.'

They waded from the water, and Helen was aware that Fenton's bold eyes took in her lithe figure. He was tall and powerful at her side as they walked up the beach to the table, and Helen was surprised to see that the strip of beach had lost almost half its narrow breadth to the encroaching tide.

'Still coming in,' Howard remarked, reaching for a towel and handing it to Helen. 'About four this afternoon should be the right time to dive to the cave. I'll take you down, Helen, if you won't be nervous.'

'I'm not afraid of the water,' she said slowly, recalling what he had said earlier about his lack of confidence in the sea. 'But I can miss this out if you'd rather not go down, or perhaps Fenton would take me.' She knew she was saying the wrong thing by mentioning Fenton, that Fenton had been angling for this situation in the hope, no doubt, of embarrassing Howard before her. Howard had risen to the bait completely, and Helen could tell by the set of his face that he had every intention of proving to her and himself that he was no longer afraid of the dive to the cave.

'We'll go down this afternoon,' Howard said firmly. 'It has been a long time since I last saw the cave, and it didn't come to mind before Fenton mentioned it again. I'm not worried about it, so we'll dive at low tide.'

A shrill whistle sounded from the top of the cliffs, and they all paused and looked upwards. Lucy was standing at the head of the steps, and she waved frantically when she saw that she had attracted their attention.

'It's me, I suppose,' Fenton said with a sigh. 'Someone must have called for me. I told her to come if I was needed. I shall have to go.' He smiled crookedly as he turned and caught Helen's eye. 'It's been nice swimming with you,' he said. 'I hope you won't forget that I've asked you to go out fishing with me sometime. I'll see you later on, and I'll go down to the cave with you in case Howard loses his nerve at the last moment.'

Howard muttered something under his breath as Fenton grinned and walked away, and Helen sensed the relief filling her as she watched the man's lithe figure ascending the flights of wooden steps. She was glad he had to go! His presence had restarted Howard's mood, and the sight of him had done something to her nerves. She sighed with sudden emotion in her, and when she glanced at Howard she saw he was staring moodily out to sea.

'He shouldn't torment you,' Helen said sympathetically.

'It isn't that so much I mind,' he replied slowly, spreading a towel and lying on his back upon it. He stared over his head at the cliffs, and Helen, spreading a towel and lying at his side, saw that he was studying Fenton's ascending figure. Lucy was waiting at the top of the cliff, and Fenton seemed in a hurry to reach the girl.

'I suppose he asked Lucy where we were,' Howard said. 'I should have told her not to say. He would have to come and spoil everything! Perhaps we should have gone to some other beach, but it is a bit thick when you can't get a little peace on a private beach.'

'He has as much right to be here,' Helen pointed out gently.

'Of course he has!' Howard removed his attention from the cliff and looked at Helen. He pushed himself up on one elbow and narrowed his eyes against the glare of the sun. 'It was a lovely swim though. I'm never going to be able to come down here again without thinking of you. Try and come whenever you have the time, won't you?'

'I promise,' Helen responded. She gazed up at him, seeing the tiny frown on his brows. He stared out at the sea, and stifled a sigh.

'I'm coming to the end of my

patience,' he said slowly. 'I shall have to move out of here and find a place of my own. I can't take much more of Fenton. He can have the estate for all I care. Grandfather will have to make his own arrangements. I don't mind, but I'm tied to this place just like one of the servants. I have my own business to run, and all this worry about Grandfather just won't do.' He sighed again and shook his head. 'Fenton is a damned nuisance! He only shows his face because he likes to spoil things. I suppose he'll be back this afternoon, worse luck!'

'You don't have to go down into that cave if you don't want to,' Helen suggested.

'Don't worry about it,' he told her firmly. 'I'm not afraid. I admit that I panicked when I was a youngster. But that was a long time ago, and since I've grown up I've had a lot of thought about Fenton. He was the one always talking about being afraid, and I was the one who always carried out the dares. I'm beginning to think that

Fenton is the coward!' He laughed harshly. 'One of these days I may get the chance to prove it to him and everyone else. I remember that Fenton never climbed that ledge you saw me on when we met.' He rolled on to one side and pointed across Helen's body with an outstretched hand. His forearm touched her bare shoulder, and Helen felt a tremor pass through her. 'Over there,' he said. 'You can see the ledge. It starts at the bottom of a small funnel leading down from the top of the cliff and edges along to that spot where I met you.'

Helen looked, and caught her breath when she picked out the ledge. It seemed to follow an unscalable path across the face of the cliff.

'Fenton doesn't know what he's saying when he calls you a coward,' she remarked. 'A man who can climb along that ledge can't be afraid of anything.'

Howard smiled. She saw the glint of his teeth. He lowered his hand and his fingers rested against her shoulder.

141

Helen did not move, and her breathing became shallow. She looked at him through narrowed eyes, and saw a host of expressions crossing his face.

'You'd better watch the sun today,' he said huskily. 'It is your first time, and if you get burned you'll be awake most of the night.' He didn't move his hand, and Helen lay looking up at him. He eased himself towards her, supporting himself on one elbow, and then he leaned over her, his face very close to hers. 'Helen, you're a very attractive girl! I'm hoping that we're going to become good friends. I lead a very lonely life, and apart from wanting to see you, your presence with me will help keep Julia off my neck. Let Fenton have her to contend with. He deserves her.'

Helen made no movement, and the pressure of his shoulder against hers was sending shivers of feeling through her. He was smiling down at her, relaxed now, his black thoughts of Fenton gone from the surface of his mind. But he made no move to kiss her, and Helen was relieved because she was afraid that he might start flirting, and that she couldn't bear, with the wounds of her affair with Gary Milton still hurting. But she wanted him to kiss her! The thought passed through her mind again, surprising her with its intensity. It was a definite sensation and she could not control it.

'I hope to get to know you really well by the time Doctor Wyatt returns,' he went on, gazing into her blue eyes. He craned closer to see his reflection in the pale depths. 'What beautiful blue eyes you've got. They're like liquid sky!' He laughed as she smiled. 'And your teeth are small and even. They don't look real, they're so perfect. You should have been a model, Helen, not a doctor.'

'That sort of life wouldn't suit me,' she retorted. 'I like to live quietly, although I can't say that a doctor's life is something of a retreat, especially when the calls come in the middle of the night.'

'But you like the work, don't you? It gives you a great feeling, I'm sure.

You're a girl in a million, Helen. I'm convinced of that, and I've only known you a couple of days. To think that before this weekend our lives never crossed. But now I feel as if I've known you for ever. You're not like a stranger. You're the nicest girl I've ever met!' He nodded slowly. 'I'm not going to pass you up. I hope you don't mind my telling this! But the reason why I haven't been out with girls so very often is because I've never liked bringing them to 'Oceanus'. Grandfather is bad enough to frighten off an angel, but Fenton is the one! I don't like to introduce girls to him.'

'Does he take them away from you?' Helen queried.

'More often than not!' He smiled tightly. 'So you've guessed! Does he have that effect upon you? Girls have told me Fenton is like a magnet. They start off by liking me, but when they meet him I take a back seat.'

'I can feel his power,' Helen admitted slowly, 'but I have no regard for Fenton.

There is something about him that repels me, to tell you the truth. My instincts warn me against him. I have always followed the guide of my conscience, and I shan't ever be more than polite to your cousin.'

'That's the nicest thing you'll ever say to me,' Howard said enthusiastically, and he bent over her and kissed her firmly on the mouth.

Helen responded immediately, and lifted her hands and placed them upon his shoulders. He slid an arm across her, holding his weight away, but letting her feel the strength in his arms. For an interminable period they remained close, their lips touching in a gentle, almost passionless kiss, but slowly Howard increased his power, and soon they were lost in the grip of tense emotion. Helen kept her eyes closed against the brilliance of the sky overhead, and her mind was suddenly blank. Thoughts were not needed in this moment of bliss, and she felt a strange relaxation filtering into her mind, as if the powerful ghost of a dead love was being forced out by a host of new and exciting emotions. Just two days ago, she thought remotely, they hadn't known of each other's existence, but already they were making an impression, one upon the other, and there was no telling where this association might lead!

7

They went up to the house for lunch, and Helen was relieved to find that Fenton had gone out to answer a call and had not yet returned. She knew Howard was entertaining similar feelings, but he said nothing, and they sat in a sunny room and ate a cold lunch. Edsel Ormond did not put in an appearance, and Helen mentioned this fact. Howard spoke to the maid when she appeared, and they were informed that Edsel Ormond had decided to spend a complete day in bed.

After lunch Howard seemed in a hurry to get out of the house, and Helen knew why. Not being eager to see Fenton again, she hurried too, and they went down to the beach to lie in the hot sun for an hour.

'Feel like another swim?' Howard demanded. 'The tide is going out now.

If you want to go down into the cave we could attempt it before Fenton shows up. I'd rather do it alone.'

'Are you sure you want to go?' Helen was doubtful. She didn't want him to panic underwater and get into difficulties. 'Why don't you get the underwater diving gear you mentioned and do it the easy way? There's no need to prove to me that Fenton is wrong about you. You're not a boy, Howard.'

'Thank you for putting it that way, but I'm not worried about Fenton's words. I should like to show you the cave. It is a wonderful sight. I think I would have made the trip again before this, but it never crossed my mind until Fenton mentioned it this morning.'

'Where is the cave?'

'Over there at the north end of the cove, just about where the beach ends. There's another bay beyond this one, and the cave is in the high ground between the two. Above the cave is the spot that's been named *Fool's Leap*.'

'Where Fenton's father drowned,'

Helen said. 'I suppose the spot has a fatal fascination for Fenton.'

'Something like that. Come on then. Let's see if the swimsuits are dry.'

Helen got to her feet and went to the rocks where Howard had spread the swimwear out in the sun before going up to lunch, and she found them dry. She went behind the rocks to change, and when she emerged, carrying her clothes, Howard took her place. When he was attired for the sea he took her hand and they walked along the shore to the north end of the cove, a matter of six hundred yards. When they had walked as far as they could Howard smiled at her.

'We'll have to swim from here,' he said tensely, despite his smile. 'There's not much of a swell today so we needn't worry about being dashed against the rocks. You see that pointed rock on the very top of the cliff? There's a flat ledge just this side of it. That flat piece is *Fool's Leap*. Well, the cave is directly below it, so we have to swim out as far as that, then dive down. I'll go first, and you'll be able to see the entrance of the cave below. Follow me in at a distance, and remember that we have to swim several yards along the tunnel before coming to the surface inside the cave. Take a nice deep breath, and once you've entered the tunnel you've got to keep going. There's not enough room to turn back.'

'Right,' Helen said. She paused and studied his face. 'Are you sure you want to go?'

'Quite sure.' He spoke stiffly, and Helen knew his nerves were tense. He cast a look back along the beach towards the steps, and Helen followed his gaze, relieved that Fenton was nowhere to be seen. 'Let's go,' he said curtly, and began to wade out into the sea. Helen followed him closely.

They swam out to the spot he had indicated, and for a moment they trod water while Howard checked their bearings. Then he nodded.

'Don't forget a nice deep breath,' he

reminded, smiling, and then he filled his lungs with air and disappeared beneath the surface.

Helen took a deep breath and prepared to follow him. She kept her eyes open as she went down, following the shimmering figure he showed to her. The water was greenish, and there were many shadowy spots in the rocky wall of the cliff. She kicked powerfully, going down and down, and the dive seemed never ending. Howard was below her, and she saw his head and shoulders disappearing into a hole that was barely large enough to permit the passage of his body. She wondered vaguely if the passing years had blocked the tunnel, and worried that if he could not get through he might panic, with her behind him blocking his way back to the surface. But he disappeared completely, and Helen clawed at the surrounding rocks to prevent herself being taken back to the surface. She swam headfirst into the hole and felt her back scraping against smooth rock as she negotiated the short tunnel.

Before she was aware of it, and certainly before she exhausted the air in her lungs, she was through the tunnel and shooting up to the surface inside the cave. She almost popped out of the water, and found herself beside Howard, treading water, gasping deeply. There was enough greenish light coming through the tunnel to permit them partial vision, and as Howard swam to the stretch of sand inside the cave, Helen gazed around with interest.

'We've got a storm lantern on a ledge in here.' Howard's voice was somewhat muffled, yet booming in the close confines.

'Where does the air come from?' Helen demanded, swimming towards him. 'The tunnel is always under water, isn't it?'

'Yes. Do you know, I've never thought about that?' His face was a blur as he turned towards her. 'But the cave goes upwards for a good way, and there's no chance of seeing where it ends. I suppose there are cracks and crevices up there that permit air to circulate. At the far end, over there, I have felt a distinct draught. I remember it quite well, because Fenton suggested that there was another entrance, or exit, somewhere. We have found evidence that someone has used the place in the past. There was even an old brandy cask floating in here. It was empty, of course.'

His tones were echoing in the gloomy space, and Helen was surprised that so much light penetrated from the sea. They left the water and Helen felt hard sand beneath her feet.

'Just a moment, Helen, and I'll light the lantern,' Howard said, disappearing into the murk as he moved away.

Helen remained in the dank stillness, looking around at the dim objects nearby. Suddenly a pinpoint of light sprang into being, and a moment later the strong flame of a storm lantern filled the cave with yellow light. Helen stared around, and it seemed to her that the walls and lofty roof of the cave were studded with jewels.

'It's beautiful,' she said breathlessly. 'I wouldn't have missed it for the world. If I had found this place years ago I wouldn't have been able to resist the impulse to explore. There might be another way in, or perhaps there's still a cache of smuggler goods.'

'I doubt it.' Howard shook his head, his shadow thick and black on the wall behind him. 'It might have been used as a hiding place by some of the smugglers, but I doubt if they would have used it for anything else. It's too difficult to get into.'

'Unless there is another entrance,' Helen prompted.

'You really are taken up with this part of the country, aren't you?' Howard's teeth glinted in the light. 'I must take you on a visit to all the places of interest. I've got a great feeling that when the time comes for you to leave us you won't feel like going.'

Helen suppressed a shiver, and he noticed.

'Are you feeling cold? It is dank in

here. Perhaps we had better be going.' He was instantly concerned. 'What did you think about the tunnel? Were you scared coming in?'

'No.' Helen smiled. 'It takes a lot to frighten me.'

'Good. I wonder if you'd like to try that ledge with me. It's not too difficult. It looks harder than it really is. Fenton would be livid if you made it, because he daren't try.'

'I don't think I'll risk my neck just to make Fenton look cowardly,' Helen said with a smile.

'Perhaps you're right, but I can't afford to miss any chance to keep even with him. It's an eternal battle between us. There has never been any war declared between us, but the hostility is there.'

'I think I have sensed it,' Helen said as he blew out the lantern, and for a moment they were silent, in total darkness until their eyes became accustomed to the gloom. 'He's a very intense man, Howard. Do you think he might get really upset if your grandfather's will doesn't suit him?'

'I've often thought about that,' he admitted harshly. 'I don't know Fenton's limits. I think he could do a lot worse than he's already done.'

'That sounds bad,' Helen said as they waded into the water. 'Shall I go first or will you?'

'You'd better go first, so I can keep an eye on you. This place is giving me the shivers now.'

'See you up top!' Helen took a deep breath and dived, kicking downwards to the greenish patch that marked the entrance to the tunnel. She skimmed through quickly, reached the open sea, and shot to the surface, and a moment later, as she was treading water, Howard appeared at her side. There was relief on his face as they kicked for the shore and waded to beach.

'Well,' he declared. 'I didn't show any sign of nerves, did I?'

'No,' Helen admitted. 'I was watching you very closely, and that dive could be something of an ordeal to a person with no real confidence in the water. If you really feel uncomfortable underwater, then you did remarkably well in taking me down there.'

'Perhaps you'll tell Fenton when you see him,' he remarked. 'It was chilly though, wasn't it? This is another world.'

The sun was strong upon them as they went back to the table and their towels, and they stretched out on the sand and enjoyed the heat. Helen drowsed, her eyes half-closed, and the sound of the waves lapping upon the shore was very soothing. She was almost asleep when a voice hailed them.

'Fenton!' Howard said instantly, and he sat up and stared at the steps as Helen opened her eyes.

It was Fenton descending to the beach, and he was dressed in his swimming trunks and sandals. Helen watched him coming towards them, and again she felt a tremor of some shadowy emotion that passed through

157

her. She didn't know what to make of Fenton. There had never been another man in her life who emitted so many impulses by the power of his personality, and Helen was not certain that all of them were good impulses. She always felt disturbed by his proximity, and judged that it could be only bad impressions disturbing her.

'Hello there,' Fenton greeted, kicking sand over Howard as he approached. 'All ready for the big dive? You don't have to come along, Howard, if you're afraid.'

'You're too late, Fenton,' Howard replied eagerly, grinning at Helen. 'We've just come back from the cave.'

'You've been down?' Fenton glanced at Helen for confirmation, and she saw an expression of ugliness flit across his smooth face. It passed so quickly that she almost imagined it hadn't shown, but he could not guard his eyes from her as he smiled. 'Well! Well! So the challenge of a woman in your life has made you rise to the occasion, has it? Pity I wasn't along with you. I was looking forward to going down into the cave.'

'Well you know where it is,' Howard said pointedly. 'But it's chilly down there, and we're only just getting warmed up again. Instead of diving, why don't we attempt the ledge? I have proved my ability over that stretch of cliff, but you have it to do, Fenton.'

'It's not the same thing,' Fenton replied, moving to Helen's side and sitting down on the beach. He leaned on one elbow and looked at her, acting as if they were alone on the beach. 'A slip could mean death on the rocks below, and I'm not a careless fool to risk my life. I have a great future ahead of me.' He smiled thinly, and his teeth glinted in the sunlight.

Helen watched him, sensing the power of his mind as he stared at her. He smiled as he picked up a handful of fine sand and let it trickle upon her bare midriff. She did not move, and it was Howard who finally broke up the situation.

'Well I've had long enough down here in the sun today,' he said grimly. He pushed himself upright and stared at Helen. 'If we're going for that drive then we'd better be going. Don't quarrel with your company, Fenton, and don't get out of your depth.'

Helen did not question Howard's statement, and she got slowly to her feet, aware that Fenton's bold gaze never left her body.

'We'll dress up at the house,' Howard said, picking up his clothes, and Helen did likewise. 'Perhaps you would like a shower before you leave. It will rinse off the salt.'

'Have a nice time,' Fenton called after them, still lying on the beach, and Helen turned to smile at him as she followed Howard up the steps.

At the top of the cliff they paused to gaze out to sea, and Helen caught a glimpse of white sails in the distance. She felt enraptured by the scene, and came back to earth only when Howard uttered an exclamation. Looking around, she saw Lucy, the maid, hurrying towards them from the house.

'Something's wrong,' Howard declared. 'She never runs unless it's urgent.'

'Your grandfather!' Helen said quickly, and they hurried towards the fast approaching girl.

The maid was breathless when she reached them, and could only gasp for some moments as Helen and Howard awaited her words.

'What is it, Lucy?' Howard demanded. 'Is it Grandfather? Is he having another attack?'

The girl nodded, and Howard set out for the house at a run, leaving Helen to follow closely. The maid tried to keep up with Helen, but she was breathless, and eventually stood waiting to regain control of her lungs. Howard disappeared into the house before Helen was anywhere near, and by the time she got into the hall the place was deserted. She paused for a moment, then went into the library, finding it deserted. She pulled on her clothes over the bikini

161

and then ascended the stairs in search of Edsel Ormond's room.

Voices were coming from a room ahead, and the door was ajar. Helen approached it and tapped gently, then peeped around the door. She saw Howard beside a large bed, and there was the housekeeper standing at the foot of it. She heard the harsh breathing of Edsel Ormond. The old man was seated on the side of the bed, leaning forward in an attempt to get relief, and Helen wasted no more time as she entered the room.

'Have you called for Doctor Wyatt?' she demanded, and the housekeeper nodded. Howard looked up at her with alarm showing on his face, and he stepped aside as Helen reached the old man. She felt his pulse and found it rapid and weak. A glance at his face showed that he was bathed in a cold sweat. His eyes were closed and his hands were tightly clenched. His complexion was blue, the face shining with sweat, and Helen spoke gently, pitching her voice above the harsh sound of his breathing. 'Do you have any treatment from Doctor Wyatt?' she demanded. 'Has he left anything with you to take when an attack begins?'

'In that drawer,' Howard said, pointing to a small bedside locker. 'There are some capsules which Grandfather has to crush in his handkerchief.'

'Amyl nitrate,' Helen said, moving around the old man to get at the drawer. She opened it and found the capsules. Howard produced a clean handkerchief and Helen took it, crushed a capsule in the folds, and held it under Edsel Ormond's nose to be inhaled. She made no attempt to alter his position, knowing that he had adopted the attitude which gave him greatest relief. He would resent any interference.

'There's nothing else I can do until Doctor Wyatt gets here,' she said softly to Howard. 'Perhaps you'd better go and get dressed. I'll stay with him now.'

Howard nodded, and thanked her as he departed from the room. The housekeeper went with him, closing the door at her back, and Helen stood beside the old man, who suddenly lay back on the bed and relaxed. He was still struggling for breath, and Helen took his pulse again, finding no change in its rate.

'At least you don't fuss me around like Wyatt does,' Edsel Ormond suddenly gasped. 'But this won't last long. It will pass in a few minutes. I often get these attacks, and if no one is around I don't bother to send for Wyatt.' He opened his eyes and stared at her, and Helen could see his complexion was returning slowly to its normal colour. 'There's a hypodermic syringe in a small case in that drawer. Wyatt gives me an injection of adrenalin for these acute attacks.'

'I think we'd better wait until Doctor Wyatt comes before treating you further,' Helen said. 'You have a heart condition as well.'

He lay still, and Helen remained standing by the bed. She heard the sound of a car approaching shortly after, and a few moments later the door of the room was opened by Howard, who stepped aside for Doctor Wyatt to enter.

'Hello, Helen,' the doctor greeted. 'I'm glad you were on the spot.' He approached the bed, setting down his bag on a convenient chair. Helen watched him as he approached Edsel Ormond, and she explained what action she had taken. He nodded, and after a few moments straightened to face her. 'He'll be all right now. It's not a sharp attack. I'll give him an adrenalin injection.'

Edsel Ormond remained lying on the bed. His breathing was still rapid, but not so laboured, and as the minutes passed he began to look better.

'Are you staying here, Helen?' Doctor Wyatt demanded.

'I'll stay as long as I'm needed,' she replied.

'Good. I want to get back. I'm expecting a call to come in. Can I leave you to take care of things here?'

'Of course.' Helen nodded.

'He should be all right now if he takes things easy.' The doctor bent over the sick man, and Helen saw Edsel Ormond move slightly.

'You can leave, Wyatt,' the old man said huskily. 'I'm quite happy in Doctor Farley's hands.'

'Goodbye then. I'm glad you've got confidence in her.' Doctor Wyatt smiled as he passed Helen, and he took up his bag and departed, calling a cheery goodbye to Helen.

Howard came back into the room, and Edsel began to ease himself up on his pillows. Helen went to his side, and he let her arrange the pillows.

'That's better,' he gasped. 'I was feeling like a fish out of water. Howard, I want you to leave me alone with the doctor. I want to talk to her. She'll let you know when I'm through.'

Howard nodded and turned to depart, and Helen caught the surprise on his face. When the door closed the old man made a motion for Helen to sit down on the chair beside the bed, and she did so.

'Listen to me,' he said hoarsely, and sweat was appearing on his forehead again.

'Please, Mr Ormond,' Helen said quickly. 'You must lie still and rest. Don't talk now. There will be plenty of time later.'

'There might be plenty of time for you,' he retorted grimly, 'but I'm an old man. I'm nearly eighty. I've had a long life, but it's almost over now. I can't lie here and rest with such an uneasy mind to spur me. I want to talk to you. As soon as I saw you on Friday afternoon I told myself that you were the one person who could help me.' He paused for breath, and Helen wiped his forehead. She listened to his words, wanting to humour him in order to quieten him. He shook his head impatiently. 'I sensed something about you, and that's why I've relented in your favour. I need help. You're a doctor, and you're intelligent. I want to put a proposition to you.'

His voice trailed off and he gasped for breath. Helen stifled the impulse to stop him. He would not obey, and she knew the best way to get him to rest was to hear him out.

'There's only one thing I'm concerned about in this world,' he went on slowly, his breath wheezing in his chest. 'This estate. There are only three Ormonds left, and one of them isn't fit to inherit. I'm talking about Howard and Fenton. Howard is the man I want to leave this place to, but I'm afraid that Fenton might do something to change my decision. Howard would be satisfied to inherit just money from the estate, but I want him to have the estate. Fenton wouldn't settle for money alone, and that's all he's going to get.'

'What can I do to help?' Helen asked gently.

'What do you think of Howard? I know you've only known him a few days, but that should be long enough for you to form some kind of an opinion. Do you like him?'

'Very much,' Helen said, taking a deep breath.

'Neither of them has married,' Edsel Ormond went on slowly, and his dark eyes seemed to hold Helen's gaze against her will. There was something of Fenton's manner in him at this moment, and she suppressed the chill sensation that spread along her spine. 'Howard won't ever marry, because he's too damned interested in that business of his. The only girls he meets are those with whom he comes into contact through his factory, and they're not the type to fit in here. But I've noticed a change in him since you came along, Doctor Farley. I had a long talk over the telephone with Wyatt on Saturday evening.'

'About me?' Helen interrupted.

'Of course. I wanted to know what kind of person you are. I'm going to change my will. I've been intending to for some time. The estate was to be sold and the proceeds shared between Howard and Fenton. I couldn't make up my mind what to do, but if Howard married a girl like you, then the family line would go on, and it seems to me that's the best thing that could happen. Fenton's children, if he had any, would be poor creatures, I'm sure. His father killed himself because Fenton's mother was insane. I'm certain Fenton has inherited his mother's mental condition. I've had him living here with me for a very long time, and I know. Howard has got to inherit! There's no other way, and I'm going to make his inheritance dependent upon one fact. He's got to marry you before he can lay claim to the estate.'

Helen was shocked by the old man's words, and speech would not come when she opened her mouth. She gulped at the lump in her throat, and then began to protest.

'But this isn't fair to Howard!' she said. 'He might in time meet a girl he could love. This way he'll have doubts, and I would think that he was being pressed into courting me because of the inheritance. You have no right to dictate the future of his life or mine.'

'He won't know about it unless you tell him,' Edsel Ormond said firmly. 'Keep it quiet by all means, and Nature, or Fate, might solve all the problems for me. But I must put it into the will just in case I die before you two get together. Don't argue that you might turn him down if he proposed. I'm an old man and I'm no fool! You two were meant for each other, and I think it will work out the way I want. I know I'm putting a burden on your shoulders, Doctor Farley, but you're a sensible woman, and I know you'll be a great ally to me. That's what I wanted to talk to you about, and now it's off my chest. I shall send for my solicitor tomorrow and have the will changed on those lines. If I have my way, Doctor, you will be the mistress of 'Oceanus' after my death.' He chuckled harshly as he relaxed and sank back on his pillows. 'Now let me sleep. I'm well satisfied with this.'

8

Helen left the room with her thoughts in a turmoil. She could understand how the old man felt about his earthly possessions, but it wasn't fair that he should involve her in his solution to the problem of inheritance. She liked Howard, but she had known him only three days, and the knowledge of what was going into the will might finally influence her feelings towards him. It would be dreadful knowing that his future, and the future of 'Oceanus' depended upon their marriage. How would she know, if she came to love him, that her feelings were not built upon the fact that she would be the next mistress here? And what of Fenton? He was an Ormond and, no matter his mental state, he was entitled by birth to a share of the inheritance!

She shook her head slowly as she

went down to the library to find Howard. Realising by the questions teeming through her mind that there was no simple answer, she could begin to appreciate the heart-searching that Edsel Ormond must have done. She tapped at the door of the library, and a moment later Howard opened it.

'How is he?'

'He's trying to sleep now,' she replied, and was aware that an awkwardness had arisen in her mind. The inheritance was already throwing a shadow across her life! She sighed. This wasn't what the old man intended. 'He'll be all right with plenty of rest.'

'That's all he ever does.' Howard sounded bitter. 'I hope I don't end my days like that. Perhaps my father was lucky to have died in the war. Being cut down in one's prime must be better than lingering on with faculties fading and physical powers going like an old battery. Age is a wicked stealer. The years take youth and vigour. You know, I'm just realising what kind of a fool I am. I'm thirty, and I've done nothing in my life but take on things that others have started. My father made the factory what it is today. Of course he had Grandfather's money backing him, but that is beside the point. I've been running that factory for quite some time, and it's exactly the same today as when I took it over. It could run itself. I don't contribute anything, except time, and for that I'm very well paid. Helen, I'm in a rut. I've been sinking down and down over the past ten years, and now I'm standing on the threshold of middle-age with nothing behind me and certainly not much ahead.'

'What's brought this on?' she demanded with a slow smile.

'You, most probably.' He laughed shortly. 'The past three days have jolted me a bit. Look at you. You're practically my age, but what you've accomplished! Your life is amounting to something! Where the devil have I gone wrong?'

'I don't think you've done so badly!' Helen watched his face, her mind filled with Edsel Ormond's words. The old man had a great problem, and he was snatching at any means to solve it. But Helen was a stranger in their midst, and it was not fair to expect her to know which of the grandsons would make the better owner of 'Oceanus'.

'Should we go out?' he demanded. 'Can he be left?'

'He'll be all right now,' Helen promised. 'I'd like to go out. There seems to be an oppressive air in this house.'

'Too many skeletons in the cupboards,' Howard said with a grim smile.

They went out for the evening, and Helen found that some of the magic of the past three days had fled, the illusion shattered by Edsel Ormond's plan. How could she fall in love with a man, knowing that her action would automatically make him become an heir to a large estate and cut off another? Fenton Ormond had a claim, and who was to say that he could not prove as able as Howard?

'There seems to be something missing

this evening,' Howard remarked as they were driving to the village later. They had spent a quiet evening, and now the heat of the day was gone and there was a cool breeze blowing in from the sea. The sky was dark, pitted with countless stars, and there seemed relief in the shadows that night was come.

'We've had a long day, and lying around in the sun is very tiring,' Helen replied.

'It's not that. You seem different, somehow. It was after Grandfather's attack. Did he say anything to you up in that room? He's a rare one for insulting people or rubbing them up the wrong way. If he does say anything that you don't like, then just ignore him. He's a very sick old man, and one has to make allowances.'

'It isn't that at all,' Helen said slowly.

'Then is it me?' he asked, glancing at her.

'How do you mean?' She felt her heart miss a beat.

'Well, we've been seeing each other

for three days now, and you must have formed some opinions about me. I know the family is a bit strange, but I've always been certain that I'm normal. I've always done normal things, except play the field where women are concerned. That seems to be the right thing to do these enlightened days.'

'I think you're a very nice person,' Helen said quietly.

'That makes two of us!' He laughed. 'But seriously, can you stick seeing me week after week until Doctor Wyatt returns?'

'I think so,' she said, smiling.

'Good. Then may I expect to see you tomorrow evening?'

'That will be four evenings in a row. I shan't be able to keep this up. When Doctor Wyatt goes next week I shall be on duty all day and every day. I shan't be able to move far from a telephone, and someone will have to know where I am every moment.'

'I won't mind coming to the doctor's house of an evening to keep you company, waiting for the telephone to ring, and I might even be prevailed upon to drive you to the patient's house. That will save you a lot of trouble learning where everyone lives, won't it?'

'I'll bear your kind offer in mind.' Helen laughed. She noted that they were reaching the outskirts of the village, and when she looked out to sea there were many small lights dancing and bobbing in the darkness. The sight made her think of Fenton Ormond and his offer of going fishing, and she shuddered as he brought the car to a halt in front of the doctor's house.

'I'll ring you tomorrow evening about six-thirty,' he said, turning to her. 'I shall know by then if I'm free from work, and you'll know if you have any duties to perform. I'm not looking forward to tomorrow, you know. This is the first week-end that I'm not glad to see the back of. You've made a wonderful change in my life, Helen.'

'So soon?' She meant to speak lightly,

but somehow her voice quivered, and she felt emotion rushing up into her throat. There was a void in her heart, a sore place that Gary Milton had vacated so callously, and new pressures were trying to fill it. She was naturally trying to prevent a repetition of Milton's power, and she was afraid that Howard Ormond might be the man best fitted for that task, and once he stepped into that void he would assume the power to hurt her or make her happy. It meant she would have to trust him, and trust was something of which she had little at the moment. But there were many aspects of the situation that had to be appraised. Edsel Ormond had imposed stringent conditions upon his heirs, and they were as yet unaware of them. Fate could solve the problems, but Helen had the feeling that the whole question of the future of 'Oceanus' had been thrust upon her slim shoulders. Her decision would give the estate to Howard or Fenton.

'I kissed you today,' Howard said

slowly. 'It's the first time I really wanted to kiss anyone. I've never met a girl like you before, Helen, and I mean that. That must sound strange, coming from a man of thirty, but it's the truth. They say it happens like that once in a while. Fate plays games with its mortal pawns. You came here and I was waiting, and we met and something happened. If you were to leave this place tomorrow you would have wrought a change for me. It's a strange fact that one person can do great things for another without ever realising the significance of it.'

Helen nodded, and his arm came out of the darkness and encircled her shoulder. She leaned against him, losing her stiffness, the fear that Edsel Ormond's words had put into her. Here was a man who felt attracted to her, and she was suffering from the same pressures of Fate. Why should she question the future? All that could be expected of her was that she did her work to the best of her ability, and if it was arranged in Heaven that she and Howard Ormond should fall in love, then it would happen, and Fenton Ormond would never get his hands on 'Oceanus'.

Howard kissed her tenderly, stirring up old feelings in her, and Helen shivered as if from cold as he gathered her close with surprisingly strong but gentle arms. His mouth against hers set up erratic impulses inside her, and threads of romance, light and elusive, yet strong and binding, seemed to coil around them. Helen felt a lightness settling upon her. This was sweet, and the man holding her was not Gary Milton. This man meant something to her, despite the shortness of their knowledge. As Howard had said, Fate sometimes played tricks upon perfect strangers, thrusting them together and cutting out the time usually needed for a man and a woman to fall in love.

'Until tomorrow, Helen,' he said jerkily, and Helen nodded happily.

'I shall be waiting for you to call,' she replied, and he kissed her again, sighing regretfully as she opened the door and slipped away from him.

When he had gone she walked into the house, and as she went to bed her thoughts were busy on new threads, and she was finding hope among her emotions. She fell asleep with her mind engaged upon all those new impressions gained over the past three days, and she was not sorry that she had left London and come to Cornwall . . .

Next morning she awoke early, intending to help Doctor Wyatt with the surgery and do some of the house calls. The day was bright, and with breakfast not yet ready she slipped out of the house and went for a walk along the little quay. There were many small boats on their way out, dotting the smooth surface of the sea, and Helen enjoyed her walk, gazing around with interest at sights that were new to her. When a voice hailed her she was surprised, and put a hand to her eyes to shade them against the glare of the sun. A tall figure came towards her, and Helen did not immediately recognise him.

'Good morning, Doctor Farley, and what are you doing out here so early in the morning?' he demanded good naturedly. 'Are you looking for someone to take you out for a couple of hours?'

'Not this morning, Mr Pacey,' Helen replied, recognising him as the fisherman who had come into the surgery with the hook caught in his hand. She noted that he had a strip of plaster over the wound. 'How is your hand?'

'Better now, I expect,' he replied, his blue eyes bold as they studied her. 'Any hope of me taking you out this evening?'

'I'm sorry, but I do have an engagement for this evening,' she replied.

'I expected you would have.' He was smiling, and Helen imagined that he didn't really want to take her out but was just amusing himself.

'Why should you imagine that?' she queried.

'You're seeing Howard Ormond. That let's men like me out of it, eh?'

'I don't know what you mean.'

'Perhaps that's as well. But you'll

183

have to go a long way to find a better man than Howard. You've picked the best one of the two.'

'You're talking of Howard and Fenton now?' Helen kept her tones even and gently pitched. She knew there would be some speculation among the villagers, and she did not want to add to the situation by sounding outraged or upset. 'I'm sure that one is as good as the other. Good morning, Mr Pacey, and take care of that wound. Don't let any dirt get into it.'

She walked away, heading back to the house, conscious that he was watching her, and she controlled the impulse to glance back at him. When she reached the house she found that Doctor Wyatt was waiting for his breakfast, and she joined him in the kitchen.

'That's a good habit to form,' he observed, studying her keenly as she joined him in the little alcove that served as a diner. 'If I were younger I'd still take a constitutional.'

'The weather is right for it,' Helen

admitted. 'I don't suppose I'd dare put my nose out of doors in the winter.'

'You'll get used to it,' he observed. 'I'm not letting you get away from here when I return, Helen. Unless I'm greatly mistaken, you're going to have to settle down in these parts. I think you should, anyway. Your ancestors lived around here.'

'What did Edsel Ormond want to know about me?' Helen asked quietly, and she saw the fleeting expression of wonder that crossed his face.

'Just the usual thing a patient wants to know about a new doctor. Why do you ask? Did he have anything to say to you last night?'

'So you do know something about his plans!'

'A doctor hears many confidences in his work,' Doctor Wyatt replied evasively. 'I think we'd better make a start with breakfast, don't you? I hate starting the day behind time.'

Helen nodded, and they ate. She was thoughtful, and after the whirlwind three days of seeing Howard she found that the thought of a whole day stretching before her without the chance of seeing him gave her a kind of breather in which to take stock. It was impossible to assess just what had happened to her in those short days. Howard had certainly attracted her, and she could not but help wondering what magic he had used to do it. She had never been light-hearted about love and romance. She hadn't been a flirt, and yet she had responded almost to his first kiss. She felt comfortable with him, and was looking forward eagerly to seeing him again. All that in the space of seventy-two hours! No wonder Edsel Ormond had thought up what he fancied was the perfect solution to his problems. Howard was normal, but needed pushing into marriage, and if that was accomplished the line of the Ormonds would continue.

After breakfast they left for the surgery, and Helen helped with the patients. But her mind was more than half occupied with thoughts of Fenton Ormond. How would he feel when he knew the contents of that new will? She compressed her lips as she thought about it, and when Doctor Wyatt left the surgery to start his round of the house calls, leaving her several from the bottom of the list, Helen reached for the telephone and called 'Oceanus'. Lucy replied, and Helen asked for Edsel Ormond.

'Hello?' The old man's voice was high pitched and weak when he spoke, and Helen could hear his breath rasping in his throat.

'This is Doctor Farley, Mr Ormond. How are you feeling today?'

'Quite well,' came the steady reply. 'Are you calling on me at all?'

'Only if you want to see me.' Helen didn't know how to put into words the thoughts running through her mind. She took a deep breath. 'I would like to talk to you about our conversation of yesterday.'

'I rather thought that you would.' He

laughed in a cackling tone. 'Why don't you come to lunch? I shall be here alone. You aren't busy this week, are you? I understood Wyatt to say that he was leaving next Monday, and knowing him, I expect he'll remain in harness until the very last moment.'

'I am helping him, getting into the routine,' Helen said slowly. 'But I'm sure I can come to lunch. What time would you expect me?'

'Twelve,' he said without hesitation. 'But talking to me won't make the slightest difference, you know. My mind is made up. My solicitor will be coming here this afternoon. You might stay to meet him. He knew your father, no doubt. Have you told Howard about my intentions?'

'Certainly not!' Helen spoke sharply. 'That would only create trouble, and I thought that was what you wanted to avoid. You won't tell either of them about it, will you?'

'Do you think that I'm a coward?' Edsel Ormond demanded. 'I don't intend dying off and having my last wishes made known to them by some unfeeling solicitor. I have a high regard for my estate, and I want both grandsons to know exactly why I'm taking this peculiar course.'

'I'll be with you at twelve,' Helen said firmly. 'Perhaps we might continue the discussion then.'

'It's not a discussion, because my mind is made up,' came the harsh retort. 'My choice is made and there is nothing further to be said about it. I shall tell both men about it after the will has been signed.'

'That won't be fair to Howard, or to me,' Helen said. 'I think there could be some sort of a future for Howard with me. I haven't known him more than three days, of course, but it doesn't take long to get to know the important things about a person. But if you don't let it evolve naturally then everything could go wrong. Make that stipulation in your will by all means, but keep it away from them.'

'Be here at twelve sharp,' the old man said urgently, and slammed down the receiver.

Helen went out to make her calls, and her mind had difficulty in remaining upon her work. She rang the doctor's house to say that she wouldn't be home to lunch, and as noon approached she became a little nervous. Finishing her calls before the appointed hour, she drove slowly towards 'Oceanus', and when she reached the big black gates across the road she found that they were open. She drove to the house and got out of the car.

She noted with a little smile that the windows of the house were open a little. Her arrival here had started quite a chain of events, she thought as she rang the doorbell. Lucy appeared in answer, smiling happily at sight of her.

'Mr Edsel is waiting for you in the library, Doctor,' the girl said. 'Mr Howard won't be in for lunch, but Mr Fenton said he'd be coming.'

'I see.' Helen couldn't prevent the

chill from striking through her, and she wondered why the mere mention of Fenton's name should affect her so. She entered the house and the maid showed her into the library.

'Come in, Doctor.' Edsel Ormond was seated by the window, which was slightly open at the top, Helen noticed, and she crossed to his side, staring out over the sea which lay in his view. He looked up at her, nodding slowly, and she could not help thinking how very old he seemed this morning. 'Would you care for a drink before lunch?'

'No thank you,' she replied, sitting down near him. 'I'd like to talk to you about this business before Fenton comes home to lunch.'

'He won't eat with us if he does,' came the sharp retort. 'We're dining alone. I'm still the master in this house, and my wishes are obeyed. You're here as my special guest. But I do want to talk to you. I've been thinking about this business since you called me earlier. Perhaps I am going about it the

191

wrong way. I've got to ensure that Howard inherits without making it too obvious that I'm manipulating the whole thing. I think it would be a great idea if I left the estate to you, on the condition that you married either Fenton or Howard. Upon your marriage the estate would go to your husband. If you don't marry either of them then you'll get nothing but a small sum of money for your trouble.'

'But that's utterly ridiculous!' Helen said firmly. 'It's the only certain way of ensuring that trouble starts between Howard and Fenton. Or is that what you want? Are you planning for the stronger of the two to get possession?'

'No,' came the sharp reply. 'It isn't that at all. I think too much of this place to have it disposed of in that way. All I'm concerned with is having 'Oceanus' going on after I'm dead. Howard must marry in order to continue the line, but I don't think he's the marrying kind, and he won't marry unless he has some strong reason to do so. You're that reason. I'm a perceptive man, and I've seen the way you've affected him in three short days. You're going to inherit 'Oceanus', Doctor Farley, and there is nothing you can do about it. Fenton will collect a large sum of money, but the estate will go to Howard, through you.'

Helen made no reply, because she could tell that he would not be swayed, and during their lunch she could not but help wondering if his mental outlook had broken down. But he regarded her steadily enough, and afterwards, when it was time for her to leave, Helen found his handshake strong and reassuring.

She went back to the village, wondering if she would see Howard that evening, and it was in her mind to mention the whole thing to him. But how could she? There would be trouble enough when Edsel Ormond died and the will become public knowledge. She could do nothing to precipitate that, and the old man's wishes were sacred.

But all the same, she felt that Fate was playing a game with her, making up for all the uneventful years she had lived and involving her with the futures of two men who were almost strangers. One she could approve of, she thought deeply, but the other! There was a dark omen in her wondering mind!

9

The week passed all too quickly for Helen, nursing as she did the secret that Edsel Ormond had bestowed upon her. She did see Howard every evening, and by the end of that week an understanding had grown up between them. But there was an awkwardness in Helen that stemmed from the knowledge she had gained in confidence, and several times she decided to speak to Edsel Ormond again to state firmly that she had no intention of being involved with his plan. She did not see Fenton at all, and wondered if he was deliberately keeping out of her way.

On the following Monday, Doctor Wyatt took his leave on what was his first absence in many years. After he had gone Helen felt the responsibility of her position, and she worked hard at keeping up the old doctor's standards.

The people had evidently accepted her with confidence, and she had no worries about the practice. Life had suddenly expanded for her, she told herself at the end of her first week alone, and now she had known Howard for more than two weeks, with the growing awareness that he was becoming very important to her.

She did not doubt that he was beginning to rely upon her company. Hardly a day went by that she didn't see him, and if they couldn't meet in the evenings, then he would arange to see her during the day. Almost against her will she began to allow her feelings to take over from her mind, and by the time she had been handling the practice alone for a month, with June almost at the end of its course, she realised that she was in love with Howard.

That should have made Edsel Ormond's new will seem easy to fulfil, but Helen wished that the conditions in it hadn't been made. But there was a chance that Edsel would change the will if he knew that romance had come between Howard and Helen, and she felt happier about the situation with that knowledge in her mind.

The second month fled as fast as June, and with July nearing its end and the weather perfect for the numerous holidaymakers visiting that part of the coast, Helen was happy with her lot. She didn't have too much work to do, and most of her spare time was taken up with Howard, who seemed a completely different man now that love had come to him. But on the rare occasions when she saw Fenton Ormond, Helen noticed that he was becoming more withdrawn and mysterious.

'Howard,' she remarked one evening when they sat in the Bentley overlooking the sea from a high cliff, 'I don't like the look of Fenton.'

'How do you mean, darling?' he demanded, glancing at her, dragging his attention from the cluster of yachts in the bay below. 'He's a very busy man with that epidemic raging. I haven't noticed any difference in him. He's always like that during this time of the year. It must be the weather!'

'I'm not so sure. He's taken a dislike to me, I'm certain. Two months ago, when I first arrived, he seemed to be certain to try and take me away from you.'

'Not from any emotion,' Howard replied with a thin smile. 'A good emotion, I mean. He probably thought that I would get to like you, and he's always made it his business to prevent me getting anything I want. But when he saw that we were obviously meant for each other he realised that he was wasting his time. Now he's probably jealous of us, and that's what's motivating him now.'

'He almost ran me off the road the other day,' she said stiffly. 'It was on that narrow stretch just out of the village. He came one way and I was going the other. He just grinned in that cold manner of his and kept going.'

'He's begun to ask a lot of questions around the house,' Howard observed. 'Several times recently he's had arguments with Grandfather about the disposal of the estate.' He shook his head. 'Grandfather hates talking about it, and I try to keep the peace, but it's getting worse and worse. The night before last Julia Anslow turned up. She hasn't been around the place for a long time. I was about to come and meet you, and Fenton had just come in from a long case. Julia has given up trying to win me over since you arrived, and she's not had much success with Fenton. He raged at her that evening, and before she left I really thought he was going to strike her.'

'He's working too hard,' Helen said. 'I don't suppose it would do any good for you to suggest that he has a medical check-up!'

'No good at all.' Howard slipped an arm around her shoulder and hugged her. 'Grandfather seems to have taken on a new lease of life since your arrival. You've had a great effect upon all of us, Helen.'

'Including Fenton,' she remarked slowly.

'It doesn't matter about Fenton. He's always been like that. Nothing ever suits him, and he's too damned hard to please! But all the same, I do feel sorry for him. He hasn't had much of a life. I wish he could meet a girl like you, Helen, and settle down.' He paused and stared reflectively out to sea, and Helen watched his profile. 'Talking of settling down,' he mused half to himself before glancing at her, 'Doctor Wyatt will be coming back in a little under the month. Have you thought about your future, Helen? Are you going to walk out of all our lives at the end of it, or will you accept a partnership and stay?'

'It depends,' Helen said slowly, watching his face for expression. 'I think Doctor Wyatt will offer me that partnership. I've done very well here in the past two months. The people have accepted me, and they won't want another stranger coming in their midst in place of me. If I'm asked to stay, then I'll do so.'

'I'm asking you to stay.' Howard

spoke huskily, and his dark eyes were bright as he regarded her. 'Helen, I can't tell you what a difference your coming here has made to my life. All I know is that I'm looking forward to the future now instead of stagnating. The business was all I lived for, but you've made me realise that there is a lot more to life. I'm in love with you! Have you guessed that?'

'I have,' Helen said slowly, and she was thinking of Edsel Ormond's new will. 'I have found a lot of feeling for you in my heart, Howard. We seemed right for each other from the very first moment, but I'm afraid for the future.'

'Why?' he demanded. 'What's the trouble? Is it me? Is my character at fault?'

'It isn't that at all! But from the very first I've had a sense of impending trouble. I can't clarify it in my own mind, so I can't hope to explain it to you.'

'That sounds bad, but it's probably just in your mind,' he suggested. 'You did tell me that you had one unhappy love affair in your life. Perhaps that's working psychologically against you.'

'Perhaps, but I'm not sure.'

'Well it doesn't affect our feelings for one another,' he said, turning to her and kissing her. 'I love you, Helen. I don't need any more time to think about it. As soon as I can get around to it I'm asking you to marry me. I know your life is more complicated than mine. You have a partnership to consider, and if you marry you will probably want to continue as a doctor. I can understand all that, but I want you to know that I shall ask you sometime in the future, so bear it in mind.'

'I'm so glad!' Helen spoke softly, gazing up into his face, and the silence of the hot summer evening pressed in closely about them. 'I love you, Howard! It happened to me the same way. I seemed to know from the very first moment that you were someone special, that you would play a prominent part in my life. The last two months have been heavenly. The future seems to be even brighter. But that black feeling refuses to leave me.'

'Don't worry about it,' he said, kissing her, drawing her into his arms and holding her close. 'It may go in time. We're doing all right, aren't we? There's nothing to worry about.'

Helen agreed, and some of her fears were quietened, but as they were driving homeward later she began to realise that most of the trouble seemed to stem from her talk with Edsel Ormond about the new will. She resolved, as she took her leave of Howard, to see Edsel the next day and talk the matter over with him . . .

After taking surgery next day, Helen telephoned 'Oceanus' before setting out to handle the house calls to make an appointment to see Edsel Ormond. The maid took the call and informed her that Edsel would be expecting her for lunch. Helen felt lighter in spirit as she did her rounds, and then, just before noon, she drove to the big house overlooking the cliffs and the sea.

Edsel Ormond looked pale when Helen was announced. She entered the library to find him seated in his favourite chair by the window, which was open, and he glanced up at her with lazy eyes.

'How are you feeling, Mr Ormond?' she demanded.

'Not too badly, Doctor. Come and sit down. I think your fresh air treatment has helped me a little.'

'You'd feel even more fitter if you took a little exercise,' she suggested, sitting down at his side. 'Why don't you take a walk around the gardens during the day? It would do you good.'

'I'm a very old man now,' he replied with a smile. 'I don't think exercise would help me. But what did you want to see me about? You haven't called and come away from your business just to check on me, have you?'

'No.' Helen spoke slowly. 'I've been worried about this new will you've made. I thought perhaps you might feel inclined to change it in view of the altered situation.'

'What's changed since your arrival here?' he demanded, and his eyes were steady upon her face.

'Last night Howard told me that he loved me. He said that in the future he would be asking me to marry him. I shouldn't be talking about this, I know, but in view of the way I feel about your new will I think you should know, and that you ought to alter the will to make it normal.'

'I see. But how do you feel about Howard?'

'I told him I was in love with him.' Helen felt a little colour coming into her cheeks, and she saw the old man smile slowly.

'Well that's fine, but it doesn't mean that you will marry. Howard may get cold feet at the last moment, but with the will forcing him to act I have no fears that he might try and slip out of it.'

'But Fenton,' Helen said. 'I do

believe that he's suspicious of the situation. He avoids me, and when I first arrived he seemed intent upon cutting out Howard.'

'I've spoken to Fenton,' Edsel Ormond said thinly. 'I've told him to keep away from you.'

Helen stared at him, unable to find speech for a moment. Then she sighed harshly and let her shoulders slump.

'So that's it! I thought there was something wrong. But you shouldn't have done that, Mr Edsel. There was no chance, as it happened, of Fenton ever winning me.'

'I wasn't sure of that,' the old man retorted grimly. 'I know what a character Fenton is, and the way he's treated some of the local girls is no one's business.'

'But what did you say to him, that he would take any notice, Mr Ormond?'

'I told him that if he expected to inherit 'Oceanus' then he would do better to look elsewhere for a wife.' The old man laughed and slapped his knee.

He stared at Helen with triumph on his wrinkled face.

'You didn't!' Helen felt horror seeping into her. 'And you have no intention at all of letting Fenton inherit this place! How could you treat him so?'

'I want the best thing done, and I don't care what means are employed to bring it about,' he replied harshly. 'When I'm dead and gone it won't matter. Howard will have the estate and Fenton will have plenty of money.'

'Will you change your will now?' Helen asked.

'No. It remains as it is written. It's my last will and testament. The estate is coming to you, and it will revert to Howard only upon his marriage to you.'

'But Fenton would take it to court, and he would probably have the will set aside on the condition that you were mentally unbalanced at the time you made it. He would probably accuse me of having undue influence over your last days.'

'I've checked that angle with the

solicitor,' Edsel Ormond said thinly. 'The will has been so worded that there is no point upon which it can be declared invalid. The estate goes to Howard upon his marriage to you, assuming that I die before this comes about. If he doesn't marry you, then the place will be sold and you will get the largest share. Half the estate goes to you and the other half will be shared between Howard and Fenton.'

'But this is ridiculous!' Helen stared helplessly at him. 'Why should you make such a stipulation?'

'Because I don't want Fenton to get his hands on the place.'

'How can he if you leave a straightforward will leaving the estate to Howard?'

'Something could happen to Howard.' The old man paused and studied Helen's intent face. 'This is a rare county for accidents. The steep cliffs, the many caves, and the isolated spots. If Howard inherited like that he would likely be dead of an accident within a month of my death. But with you on the scene the matter is changed completely. If Howard died while married to you, then the estate would pass on to you. Fenton would be out of line. Your children would come before him. I took this course when I realised that you and Howard might get together because it's the greatest safeguard I can make to ensure the future of the estate. Marry Howard as soon as you can. The day you do marry him I'll tear up that will and write another. But until that happens the will stands.'

Helen was silent during the lunch, and afterwards she broached the subject again. But Edsel Ormond was adamant. When she took her leave he smiled at her.

'Don't worry so much about it. By handling it like this I've ensured that nothing untoward will happen to Howard. You should be grateful for that.'

'I'd like to know what you mean by an accident happening to Howard,' she retorted. 'What kind of an accident?'

'I don't really have to tell you, do I?' he countered. 'I know my grandsons better than anyone. Howard has no cause to study the situation, but I have done so because I have not much future left, and I must look beyond my death for the future of 'Oceanus'. I can say no more than that. Just don't put yourself into a situation where Fenton can act precipitately. Watch out that Howard doesn't walk too near to the cliffs at night.'

'I can't believe that you're serious,' Helen said quickly, and her heart was beating faster than normal.

'I've never been more serious in my life,' the old man retorted.

Helen left the house with her thoughts in a whirl. But she could not believe that Fenton would go to such extremes to get hold of the estate. She heard a car approaching, and paused as she was about to enter her own. She saw Fenton coming along the drive, and took a deep breath as she waited for him to pull up beside her.

'Good afternoon,' she called as he got out of his car.

'Hello,' he retorted, coming towards

her. His face was set in harsh lines, and Helen noted that his eyes were bright. 'I've been wanting to see you for quite some time. You're an extremely busy person, and when you have been here at the house I've always been out myself.'

'I've heard that you've been working hard with an epidemic on your hands,' she replied.

'That's right, but the worst of it is over now.' He took a deep breath. 'What have you called here for? Is the old man ill?'

'No. I wanted to see him. Doctor Wyatt asked me to keep an eye on him.'

'Then it must be about the will.'

Helen stared at him, not knowing how to reply. But he said nothing more, and his dark eyes bored into her.

'The will?' she repeated.

'You think I don't know about it?' He laughed. 'Edsel doesn't want me to inherit. He thinks I'm insane, like my mother!'

'You must be joking!' Helen didn't like the onus placed upon her by Edsel

Ormond's action. She felt guilty because she had been involved against her will, and her conscience was troubling her.

'Oh no!' He was still smiling, but there was a sharp expression on his handsome face. 'I wouldn't joke about a thing like that. All my life I've looked forward to inheriting 'Oceanus' because I'm the son of the eldest son. Edsel wouldn't have got this stupid idea if you hadn't come along. And you've been making up to Howard from the very first moment. I suppose that old fool Wyatt primed you to the situation before you started looking around. I suspect that Wyatt is in this plan somewhere. He and Edsel were always talking together around the house. No doubt your coming here at all was Edsel's idea, after he'd learned about you. It's common knowledge that Edsel is afraid I'll marry in case my children turn out to be half-witted.'

'I'm sure you're quite mistaken,' Helen said quickly. She didn't like the expression in his dark eyes. His voice was low pitched and intense, and his hands were trembling. I'm afraid this has nothing to do with me. My only concern is for Mr Ormond's health, and I hope you will see it that way.'

'I don't believe you. There's a conspiracy going on here, and I've just about got the rights of it. I won't let them rob me, I can tell you. I've been at the old man's beck and call too long to let this place slip through my fingers. I thought you would have had more sense, anyway, tying in with Howard instead of me. I could make you the next mistress of 'Oceanus'.'

'I'm not in the least interested about that sort of thing,' Helen replied with trembling voice. 'I have quite enough on my plate without taking on additional complications. Now if you will excuse me, I'll be on my way. I have a lot of work to do.'

He smiled grimly, and Helen got into her car. He leaned an elbow on the side of the vehicle as Helen switched on the engine.

'You may be sorry one day that you didn't find me more attractive than Howard. He's never going to get hold of 'Oceanus', no matter what the old man has got in mind. I'll fight all the way to get what I want, and I feel that I should inherit the estate.'

Helen suppressed a sigh as she drove away, and glancing into the rear-view mirror, she saw Fenton standing in the driveway and staring after her. The ugly sound of his voice alarmed her, and she recalled her disbelief of Edsel Ormond's words about Howard meeting with an accident if Fenton found out that the estate was going to Howard. She hadn't believed it at the time, but after hearing Fenton's vibrant tones she was not so sure that the old man had been dreaming.

She did not stop to close the gates behind her as she drove back to the village to continue her calls, and the afternoon passed slowly, as if time had halted its progress in order to worry her still further. She had to ring Howard at six to find out if he would be leaving the factory, and she was more than half decided to tell him everything. She could not carry the burden placed upon her mind and still retain her sharpness. She wanted nothing to aggravate her thoughts, and the Ormond family were beginning to do just that.

At six she put the call through, and spoke to Howard, and the sound of his voice was pleasant to her ears. He would be free to pick her up at seven, he told her, and Helen spent the better part of the remaining hour preparing to go out for the evening. But when Howard called she still hadn't firmly decided to tell him everything.

She was afraid that Howard might think a proposal of marriage coming from him after learning of the old man's will would seem as if he was intent upon picking up the estate at any cost. She knew him well enough to realise that he would be sensitive about it, and she didn't want anything to spoil the even throb of their lives, because in a very short time Doctor Wyatt would be coming back and she would have to make the most important decision of her life. If she agreed to stay on here and then Howard found that he couldn't marry her because of his grandfather's will she would be in an unenviable situation. She was very thoughtful as she went out to the car, and tried to shrug away her fears as Howard greeted her.

'You're looking very grim,' he declared as he leaned sideways and kissed her, and Helen smiled as she tilted her face to him. 'Have you had a very busy day? I'll call off this evening if you're feeling tired.'

'No,' she said fervently. 'I'm quite all right, and looking forward to the evening. It has been a trying day, I'll admit, but I have to expect that. Anyway, Doctor Wyatt will soon be coming back, and then I can relax for a week or two.'

'I want to get something settled between us before you have to make a decision about the partnership Doctor Wyatt will offer you,' Howard said brightly, and his dark eyes were glinting with high spirits as he studied her face.

'Well there's no time like the present,' Helen told him quickly.

'All right.' He took a deep breath and tensed, and Helen felt her heart miss a bit as he prepared to speak. She had a fancy that she knew what was in his mind. 'Helen, I want you to marry me!'

'I — ' Helen broke off as she quelled the impulse to reject him out of hand. She wanted to say yes, but she could not bring herself to do so, fearing that a public announcement now might goad Fenton into doing something criminal. But she was still half inclined to disbelieve all that Edsel Ormond had said and intimated. Surely it wasn't at all like that! But she was not so sure, and she didn't want to start a train of events that might end in tragedy.

'Listen, you don't have to give me an answer right now,' Howard said quickly, taking her hand and squeezing it. 'I just want you to know now how I feel. The decisions can come later. I think we'd better hang fire for some time because I'd like Grandfather to get used to the idea of having you around before we spring anything upon him. How does that sound, Helen?'

'Fine,' she replied, mentally keeping her fingers crossed. 'Ask me again after Doctor Wyatt's return. I shall have a great decision to make then, and after we've talked things over I shall be in a better position to know what to do.'

He left it at that, and Helen was satisfied, but she could not dispel the gloom that invaded her, or keep her thoughts from Fenton Ormond. Was the shiver of anticipation inside her just that, or a sense of premonition? She kept wondering, and her mind knew no rest . . .

10

As the following day passed uneventfully Helen began to lose some of her dread, and the next time she met Fenton he gave no indication of his feelings. Howard never spoke about the estate or mentioned the subject of wills and inheritance, and she was glad that Fenton hadn't gone out for a complete showdown between himself and his grandfather. Edsel Ormond surprised her by showing an interest in walking around the gardens, as she had suggested, and upon one occasion, when she visited 'Oceanus' to check on him, she found the old man standing in the sunshine, leaning on a stick and staring around with a proprietory air.

'I'm glad to see you out and about,' Helen told him, pausing before him, and he smiled crookedly at her, his dark eyes filled with the brightness of an inner feeling.

'I'm doing very well,' he replied. 'I'm glad I took your advice. Perhaps I should have listened to Wyatt a long time ago. I feel as if I've taken on a new lease of life. But enough of me. I want to talk to you, and I had a feeling you would be calling this morning. I was going to ring you at lunch time if you hadn't shown up.'

'You've changed your mind about your will,' Helen said quickly, and he smiled tightly.

'Just listen and I'll tell you,' he replied sharply, and Helen smiled. She was getting used to him now. 'I've had another will made out,' he said. 'No doubt my solicitor is beginning to wish that I would hurry up and die, the extra work I'm putting upon his services.'

'Not a bit of it,' Helen contradicted. 'Your last wishes should be respected.'

'That's it exactly,' he retorted. 'Perhaps you'll remember that in future. Anyway, this new will leaves you out of it completely. It will be straightforward, as if you didn't exist, and it will come into force if you should marry Howard before I die. If, on the other hand, I pass on before that happy event, then the other will takes effect.'

'What's brought on this change of thought?' Helen demanded.

'Howard's attitude towards you. I'm sure he's going to propose before very long. I had a good talk with him the other evening, and although he didn't put it into so many words I could read well enough between the lines of his conversation. You're going to be the next mistress of 'Oceanus', whether I will it or not.'

Helen smiled, but there was a picture of Fenton's face in her mind, and it filled her with disquiet. She didn't know him well enough to form an opinion of his character and mental outlook, but there were certain signs on him that gave rise to some anxiety. She shook herself from her thoughts, to find the old man staring at her, a thin smile on his tight lips.

'Why aren't you wearing some kind

of hat?' she demanded. 'This sun is rather strong. You don't want to get sunstroke!'

'I can't find my hat,' he replied sternly. 'I have an old deerstalker that I used when I was a young man. I wouldn't be seen dead in any other. But I haven't been out for years, and I don't know where the damned thing is.'

'Ask the maid to look for it,' Helen told him.

'Yes, Doctor.' He spoke so meekly that Helen glanced quickly at him, and she saw the smile on his wrinkled face.

'You've taken on a new lease of life, Mr Ormond,' she told him.

'Of course, and it's all thanks to you. When I think of all the times I argued with Wyatt about bringing in a woman doctor! I wish you had come sooner!'

'Doctor Wyatt will be pleased to hear that,' Helen told him. 'Now I must go. I have some more calls to make.'

'Are you seeing Howard later?'

'Yes,' she replied. 'I see him almost every evening.'

'I'm glad to hear it. We'll be having Wyatt back in a couple of weeks, won't we? What are your plans, if I may make so bold?'

'I'm expecting to be offered a partnership. Doctor Wyatt will be retiring pretty soon, I think. His general health is not too good, and he feels that he's done all he can for this community. If he thinks I'm capable of taking over, then I shall get my chance.'

'And if you become mistress of 'Oceanus'? What then? Will you continue to be a doctor? Would that suit Howard?'

'I'm afraid there are a lot of questions to be asked and answered before a satisfactory situation can be arranged.' Helen laughed as she turned away. 'But I promise to keep you fully informed, Mr Ormond.'

'Do that. It's more important than you realise,' he said, and turned and hobbled away, leaning heavily upon his stick.

Helen watched him for a moment,

and a shadow seemed to have fallen across her. She shook her head slowly as she turned away and walked back to her car, and as she climbed into the vehicle the sound of the barking dogs in their cages at the rear of the house pierced her awareness, and she shivered involuntarily. As she drove away she glanced back across one slim shoulder, and told herself that the big house, standing silent and brooding in the bright sunlight, did not look half so forbidding now. But there was a dark shadow in the background, and it answered to the name of Fenton Ormond . . .

Helen finished her work, and prepared to go out for the evening. She had promised Howard that she would go up to the house to see him, and as she drove along the road that led to the big house on the cliffs she felt her heart lighten and her spirits soar a little. What a difference had come to her life in two months! How had she ever managed to exist without knowing Howard? She smiled as she reached the big black gates, and she found them closed. Heaving a sigh, she got out of the car and approached the gates, but before being able to turn the handle a figure appeared from the end of the wall that abutted the gates. It was Fenton, and he was looking grim and fierce as he approached. At his side was a large black and fawn Alsatian dog, and the animal showed its teeth at Helen in a silent, frightening snarl. The animal was not on a leash, and Helen caught her breath as Fenton started opening one of the gates.

'Seeing Howard again?' he demanded urgently. He laughed, and came through the gate, turning his head to speak commandingly to the dog. The animal dropped flat and remained motionless, its dark eyes fixed upon Helen with unblinking stare, and she could tell by its suppressed animation that it was just awaiting the order to attack her. It kept showing its teeth in a silent, hideous snarl, and Helen found that more frightening than the frenzied barking that usually emanated from the wire cages at the back of the house.

'Is Howard at home?' she asked, tearing her thoughts and attention from the dog.

'Naturally! Why don't you walk up to the house and ask for him?'

'I prefer to drive up,' she replied. 'Would you open the gates for me, please?'

'Certainly, but only after I've had a little chat with you. I'm one of the two heirs to this estate, and I'm being kept in the dark about certain things. You're an outsider, Helen, but you've been taken into confidence, and you know a damned sight more than I do. I don't like that. Why should I become an outsider?'

'I'm sure that's not the situation at all,' Helen replied, half-turning to walk back to her car, but he reached out a hand and took hold of her arm in an unbreakable grip. The dog made a furtive movement forward to the gate, and uttered a low, menacing growl.

'Sit down,' Fenton snapped, and the dog subsided. 'Now,' he resumed, 'tell me what's going on, Helen. You'll agree that I have a perfect right to know.'

'To know what?' she countered.

'To know what's going on behind my back. It's my future that's been manipulated. I know you're on Howard's side. You and he are trying to get around the old man.'

'That's ridiculous, and you know it,' Helen replied with some spirit. 'I am the family doctor, and I've confined my activities around the house to just that.'

'Some doctor, the way you've taken on with Howard.'

'That's something different,' she said almost angrily. 'I am permitted a private life, you know, the same as you and anyone else.'

'You're trying to get me away from the point,' he said firmly. 'I want to know all about the old man's will.'

'Then I suggest you go and ask him about it. I have nothing whatever to do with that sort of family matter. If Mr Ormond won't tell you, then why not approach his solicitor?'

'You know perfectly well that he won't divulge anything.'

'Then why ask me? I'm a doctor, and I have sealed lips about patients and their personal lives. It's no use trying to scare me, Fenton. I won't stand for that.'

'Trying to scare you?' He looked surprised, but there was a thin smile on his stiff lips. 'That's the last thing I would do. How am I scaring you?' He dropped her arm, and Helen could feel where his fingers had pressed the soft flesh. 'I'm sorry I touched you. It was an unconscious act, I assure you. You're not my type, Helen.'

She glanced at the dog, and he saw the direction of her gaze. His smile broadened, and then he laughed.

'So you're afraid of my dog. It's surprising how many usually fearless people are afraid of dogs like *Master*. But he's not to be confused with those other dogs kept in the cages at the back of the house. This is my dog, and he's a big pet. He's not ferocious.'

'Then he's a marvellous actor,' Helen said thinly. She took a deep breath and walked back to her car, heaving a sigh of relief as she got in behind the wheel. Fenton had not moved, and she stared at him for a moment. 'Would you mind opening the gates for me?'

He nodded, his face like an impassive mask, and Helen could not prevent a shudder from rippling through her. It was as if someone had walked over her grave! He still did not move, and she could sense the sudden indecision in him. Then he took a deep breath and came alive.

'I shall be seeing you again, when you're not in full view of the house,' he said firmly. 'You can expect to see me soon.' He turned on his heel and quickly opened the gates, and the dog sprang clear, narrowly avoiding being struck. Helen clenched her hands upon the steering wheel as she drove forward.

He stood to one side, smiling mockingly, and when she had passed him, Helen surveyed him in the mirror, wondering what there was about him that struck all the warning chords in her mind. When she spotted the dog, crouching silently on the grass verge, her breath almost froze in her throat, and she sighed as she drove on to the house.

Howard was waiting at the door when she stopped the car in front of the steps, and he came down towards her, his face unusually grim.

'Is there anything wrong, Howard?' she demanded.

'There was a flaming row this evening, Helen,' he replied. 'Fenton again. He's always on at Grandfather these days. I had to speak quite sharply to him at tea, and I fancy that was what he was waiting for. He tore into the both of us with fury, and really, I don't know what it was all about. But Grandfather seems to be a different man these days. He used to upset himself with arguing, but this time he didn't. He gave Fenton as good as he got, and I do believe that he won the day when it was all over. I saw you talking to Fenton down at the gate. What kind of a mood is he in now?'

'He seemed the same as usual to me,' Helen replied, and turned to stare down the driveway. She couldn't see Fenton now, and the big black gates were closed. 'I do wish these arguments would cease. Your grandfather may not be showing any outward signs of distress, but I assure you that scenes and emotional upsets are definitely bad for him.'

'I know, and that's what makes me so angry!' Howard spoke with great feeling. 'I've remonstrated with Fenton, but he doesn't seem to care. I wouldn't put it past him to be trying deliberately to worsen Grandfather's condition.' He narrowed his dark eyes as he stared into the sun. 'Would you rather stay around the house this evening?' he demanded suddenly. 'I don't feel like going out and leaving this situation. Fenton may start again while I'm gone, and if I'm not around to curb Grandfather then things might get out of hand.'

'I have no wish to go anywhere in particular,' Helen told him. 'Why don't you show me around the grounds? We've never covered the entire estate before, and I'd like to look it over.'

'We can drive around if you like. There are gravelled paths wide enough for a car. But there isn't much to see. There is plenty of grass and a lot of trees, and that's about all.' He smiled, and Helen could see the tension leaving him.

'Shall we use my car?' she asked.

'It is smaller than my Bentley.' He laughed. 'You drive.'

They got into her car, but before she could move off a voice hailed them from the door of the house, and Helen was surprised to see Edsel Ormond waving to them.

'Hello, Grandfather? What do you want?'

'I want to come with you,' the old man said strongly. 'I don't care where you're going. I just want to get out of this house for a while.'

'Glad to have your company. You haven't been out of the house in years!' Howard glanced at Helen.

'Well that's all you know!' The old man laughed heartily as he came down the steps, leaning on his stick. 'Ask Helen about it. She talked me into it. I've been walking in the gardens for days now, getting some use back into my old legs.'

'Is that right?' Howard demanded, his face showing amazement.

'Quite right. Don't you agree that he's looking better?'

'I do. But what kind of magic do you use to get him to do what you want? Doctor Wyatt will have a fit when he learns about this.' Howard started back up the steps to meet Edsel Ormond, and Helen opened the back door of the car for the old man to get in.

She was facing into the car when she

heard Howard shout in alarm, and then there was a terrible growling sound. Swinging around, Helen was shocked to see a large dog leaping at Edsel Ormond, and before she or Howard could move the animal had struck the old man and borne him to the ground. For the space of a shocked heartbeat they stood staring at the dog savaging the man, and Edsel uttered a screeching cry of pain and fear. Then Howard rushed forward, grabbing at the dog and exerting his strength to pull it away. Helen followed him, hardly aware of what was happening, and she was horrified to see that the dog was trying to sink its teeth into Edsel Ormond's throat.

Howard threw himself upon the frenzied animal without thought for himself, and Helen rushed in to pick up the walking-stick the old man had dropped. Howard looped an arm around the dog's neck and squeezed quickly, but the dog was large and powerful, and took little notice of him. Helen thrust the end of the stick into the dog's jaws as it tried to take a fresh hold upon the old man, and she succeeded in transferring the animal's attention from Edsel to Howard.

The dog was growling ferociously in its throat, the whites of its eyes showing, and foam spattered from its jaws. Helen kept the end of the stick in the animal's mouth, and Howard was hard put to keep the bared fangs from sinking into his own throat. Edsel Ormond lay still, with blood streaking his face, and Helen could do nothing more than throw a quick glance at the old man.

'What the devil is going on here?' The voice yelled at the top of its power, and Helen glanced up and saw Fenton rounding the corner of the house. He paused for a moment, then came at a run towards them, the Alsatian which had been with him at the gate bounding along behind.

'Quick, Fenton, do something!' Howard shouted. 'This animal is intent upon tearing Grandfather to pieces.'

Helen noticed that the dog was trying to get back at the motionless old man, and she caught her breath as Fenton stepped in fearlessly and took hold of the animal by the scruff of its neck. The muscles in his forearms stood out as he exerted his strength and lifted the animal bodily from the ground. It writhed and snarled and growled impotently, and Howard got quickly to his feet, taking the stick from Helen.

'Look after Grandfather,' he said in gasping tones, and Helen saw blood on his hands where the dog had caught him. His face was pale and he was badly shocked.

'I can handle this animal,' Fenton said through his teeth. 'Keep away and I'll be able to quieten it. How the devil did it get out of its cage?'

'How would I know?' Howard retorted through compressed lips. 'Get it away from here, for God's sake, Fenton!'

Helen waited no longer, but turned to the old man, and she was appalled to see blood on Edsel Ormond's throat.

She dropped to her knees quickly, unmindful now of the snarling dog being hauled away by a powerful Fenton. Howard came to her side, and his breath was rasping in his throat as he tried to regain control of his shocked senses.

'Is he badly hurt?' he demanded, his shoulders heaving.

'I don't know, but you'd better hurry into the house and call an ambulance,' she replied. 'Then bring some clean cloths and a blanket. Hurry, Howard. If he's not badly bitten, he'll be deeply shocked. This will probably bring on an attack of asthma.'

He got to his feet and reeled towards the house, and Helen quickly examined Edsel Ormond, who was unconscious. She didn't like the look of the blueness creeping into the man's pallid face, and when she examined the blood she found that he had been bitten severely on one cheek. But vital spots had been missed by those terrible fangs. She was conscious of great relief as she checked the rest of him for damage, and found that their prompt action had prevented a tragedy. But would Edsel Ormond be able to withstand the great shock? Helen tightened her lips as she did what she could, but without her medical bag and drugs there was little in the way of first-aid that could be applied. Shock was the greatest factor now, and she knew that immediate treatment was necessary.

Howard returned, having collected a sheet and a blanket, and he dropped to his knees beside Helen, his hands trembling uncontrollably.

'Lucy is calling for an ambulance,' he said. 'I don't think they'll get here very soon. It's five miles from Radmin. Is there anything we can do?'

'I'd like to give him a shot of morphia,' Helen said. 'Shock is what we have to worry about, Howard. He has been bitten, and severely, but it's the shock that will affect him.'

'That damned dog.' Howard's voice shook as he spoke, and Helen finished covering the old man with the blanket before looking up at Howard's angry face.

'You're shocked, too!' Helen declared.

'Who wouldn't be?' he demanded, glancing down at his hands. 'But at least we prevented it from tearing Grandfather to pieces!'

'Let me look at your hands,' Helen commanded, taking hold of them, and she saw that he had been bitten several times. 'I think you'll need hospital treatment, Howard.'

'It doesn't matter about me,' he replied tensely. 'Poor Grandfather!'

Helen tended the old man, whose eyes had flickered open, and she took his pulse and checked his breathing. She was afraid that the shock he had suffered would precipitate an attack of asthma, and her trained mind told her without need of thought that his heart condition made this incident doubly serious.

The ambulance arrived within fifteen minutes, and when Edsel Ormond had been placed inside Helen and Howard went with him to the hospital, Howard travelling in the ambulance and Helen driving her car. At Radmin, Edsel was quickly taken into the Casualty department, and Helen's responsibility towards him was gone temporarily. Howard was looking very shaken, and when he was called in for treatment he smiled crookedly at Helen. He was given an injection and his wounds were dressed. When he returned to Helen he looked ghastly, and Helen knew he was more than ready to get home and go to bed, but they had to wait for a verdict upon Edsel.

Within twenty minutes a doctor appeared, and he informed them that Edsel would have to remain in the hospital for observation.

'The bites aren't all that serious,' the doctor told them, 'but in view of his age and condition I think it wiser to hold on to him for at least twenty-four hours.'

'Helen, is there anything else that can be done for him?' Howard asked.

'I'm afraid not,' she replied gently. She knew that secondary shock would strike the old man in twenty-four hours, and that was when the real crisis would start, but she did not tell Howard.

'Has this incident been reported to the police?' the hospital doctor asked.

'Not yet. I'll do that later,' Howard said grimly, and Helen heard him sigh.

They waited until Edsel Ormond was ready to be wheeled into a ward, and saw him before he was taken away. He looked thin and very old as he lay under the blankets, and his eyes were closed, part of his face hidden by the dressing applied to the wounds. Howard took the old man's hand for a moment, and then turned away, hurrying out of the hospital with Helen following him, and she said nothing as they got into her car and she prepared to drive back to 'Oceanus'. They were both silent until the big house came into view.

'Helen, thank you for what you did,' Howard said suddenly, gazing at her with narrowed eyes. 'It wasn't a pleasant thing.

But there's more unpleasantness to come. I'm going to tackle Fenton now. Those dogs will have to go. Grandfather never wanted them here in the first place. They're not like ordinary dogs. I've never seen a more ferocious bunch. They're more like wild animals, and it wouldn't surprise me if Fenton deliberately made them so.'

'Are you joking?' Helen demanded, and he glanced at her with a wondering expression dawning on his pale face.

'No, I'm not! But I hope I'm wrong! I'm certainly going to find out.' He got out of the car when Helen stopped before the house, and shut the door quickly. 'You'd better go home now, Helen,' he said. 'I'll feel much happier if you weren't here.'

'Nonsense,' she replied. 'I'd like to know what has been happening. How did that dog escape from its cage, and why did it attack Mr Ormond and not me or you?'

'Perhaps Fenton can tell us,' Howard said grimly, and looked down at his bandaged hands. 'I'm not in such a good state to get anything out of him, but I'm certainly going to try.'

11

Helen felt frozen inside as she followed Howard. They entered the house, and in the library he paused to pour himself a stiff drink of whisky. Helen refused his offer of a drink, and moved to the window to stare out at the sea while Howard rang for Lucy. When the girl came in she asked after Edsel Ormond.

'He's deeply shocked, and will have to stay in hospital for at least twenty-four hours,' Howard said grimly. 'Where is Fenton, Lucy?'

'I haven't seen him, Mr Howard. After you left for the hospital I came into the house and kept all the doors shut, just in case any more of the dogs escaped.' The girl paused, and turned a frightened face towards Helen before continuing. 'If those dogs don't go, then I shall give my notice, Mr Howard. I'm not staying here a minute longer than I have to.'

'Don't worry, Lucy, those dogs are going,' Howard said.

'They're worse during the day,' the maid went on. 'When Mr Fenton goes out back to train them they're snarling and growling like lions.'

'Train them?' Howard demanded. 'What do you mean train them?'

'I've seen Mr Fenton in the cages with some of the dogs, and especially with the one that attacked Mr Edsel. I didn't like to disagree with Mr Fenton, because he is a vet, but I thought the way he was training that dog made it more vicious instead of teaching it obedience.'

'I see. Well thank you, Lucy, that will be all. I assure you the dogs will be gone by tomorrow.' Howard followed the girl to the door, and excused himself, leaving quickly. Helen suppressed a sigh as she awaited his return. She could hear the dogs barking at the rear of the house, and shuddered as she recalled the horrifying moments when the big dog had been attacking Edsel Ormond.

When Howard returned he was carrying a shotgun, and his pale face was set in harsh lines.

'Howard, you can't do that!' Helen went forward and took his arm. He smiled slowly.

'Don't worry,' he said briefly. 'I'm not going to shoot the dogs. It's just for my protection. I'm going round there to see what Fenton is up to, and to give him orders to get rid of the dogs by tomorrow. If my suspicions are correct anything can happen.'

'Oh no!' Helen stared at him in disbelief, unwilling to believe what his words had planted in her mind.

'You don't know the half about Fenton,' Howard said bitterly. 'I want you to stay here, Helen. It might not be safe for you.'

'I'm coming with you,' she replied resolutely. 'Don't try to dissuade me, Howard.'

He nodded slowly and turned to leave the room, and Helen kept close behind him as he went through to the kitchen. They left the house by the back door and crossed the yard to walk to the spot where the cages held the dogs. There was no sign of Fenton.

The dogs started leaping at the wire as they walked along the row of cages, and Helen kept well away. Howard paused in front of an empty cage, and his dark eyes were bright and alert as he stared at a spot where a small hole had been forced in the wire very close to the ground.

'That's where the dog got out,' he commented, squatting to take a closer look, and Helen crouched beside him. 'This is the cage where that dog was kept.' He glanced along the cages, and nodded. 'Fenton has put it in that one at the end. You don't think he infected it with rabies before turning it loose on Grandfather, do you?'

'Howard, you're not serious, are you?' Helen stared at him, and knew by his expression that he was not joking. 'Surely he wouldn't do such a thing!'

'I'm wondering why the dog attacked Grandfather and not me! I was nearer to it when it came around the corner.' He straightened and opened the cage door, stepping into the small pen, the shotgun tucked under one arm, and Helen shivered as she glanced around at the other cages, where the dogs were leaping and snarling and barking.

Howard walked around the cage, and bent to glance into the small wooden kennel in the far corner. Helen saw him reach into the kennel, and when he straightened again he was holding a small bundle of cloth in one hand. Helen studied his face as he came towards her, and the coldness inside her seemed to turn to ice. She glanced at his hand, wondering what it was that he held, and when he reached her he lifted the object up before him.

'Do you know what this is?' he demanded, and his voice trembled. Helen stared at the cloth, which was tattered and torn into shreds. She shook her head. 'It's Grandfather's old hat! His deerstalker! What the devil is it doing in here?'

Helen stared at him in silence, not liking the thoughts passing through her mind. She was recalling that Edsel had mentioned the deerstalker to her, and said something about it being lost. How had it got into the dog's cage? There was only one solution, and the thought of it horrified her.

'I think you'd better call the police immediately,' she said at length, and Howard nodded slowly.

'You're thinking what I'm thinking,' he said tightly. 'I have grave suspicions that Fenton has been training this dog, but not for obedience. He's used this deerstalker to give the animal Grandfather's scent, and that's why the dog made straight for him when it got out of the cage.' He walked to the hole in the wire and bent to examine it more closely, and when he straightened again his face was wearing a terrible expression. 'I thought at first the wire had rusted through, that the continual leaping and jumping had strained the wire and finally broken it through, but that wire has been cut. The ends are quite bright and clean. That dog was deliberately freed, Helen!'

She nodded slowly. It certainly seemed that way to her. She looked down at the hole where the dog had forced its way out of the cage, and walked closer to examine it for herself. She had to agree that the wire had been cut, and as she straightened she caught a glimpse of movement at the far end of the cages. Her heart seemed to miss a beat when she saw Fenton coming towards them, the big Alsatian he'd had with him at the gate earlier at his heels.

'Here he comes,' she said quickly, and Howard stepped out of the cage and put himself a little in front of her, facing his cousin, his bandaged hands gripping the shotgun.

'What are you doing here?' Fenton demanded as he came up. He halted several feet from them, and the big dog sank to the ground without being told, watching Helen with intent gaze, and she fancied its body was tensed and ready to spring into action. But Fenton was watching Howard, and there was open hatred upon his tanned face.

'I'll tell you,' Howard said thinly. 'These dogs have to be gone by tonight.'

'Impossible! They're my property and they're staying.'

'How did that dog get out of its cage?' Howard demanded.

'You've been taking a close look around, so you know,' Fenton replied. 'I check that wire regularly, but there must have been a weakness in it that couldn't be detected. How is the old man?'

'Are you really interested in his welfare, or are you hoping that I'll say the shock was too much for him and he's dead?' There was iron in Howard's tones, and Helen found herself taking a deep breath.

'What the devil are you saying?' Fenton demanded, his face darkening, and he made an imperceptible movement with his left hand, bringing the

251

big dog moving forward a few feet.

'If that dog makes a move towards us I shall shoot it dead,' Howard said firmly. 'Put it away in a cage.'

'He doesn't belong in a cage,' Fenton said. 'He's not like this lot. He's my dog.'

'Can you explain this?' Howard released his hold on the gun, using one hand to steady it, and with the other he tossed the remains of the deerstalker towards Fenton, who caught it and looked at it.

'What is it?' Fenton demanded, throwing it to the ground.

'You know perfectly well what it is. Grandfather's deerstalker. How did it get into the dog's cage?'

'I haven't the faintest idea.' There was no expression on Fenton's face, but he was tense, and his eyes never left Howard. 'Are you accusing me of anything?'

'What is there to accuse you of?' Howard countered, and smiled grimly when Fenton made no reply. 'A guilty mind needs no accusing. You know very well what happened. You gave this hat to that dog because it has Grandfather's scent on it. That's why the animal attacked Grandfather. You've been tormenting that dog, making it savage, and all the time it could smell Grandfather. You knew Grandfather had started taking daily walks on Helen's orders, and you planned to let that dog loose on him one day. I suppose you thought this evening was as good a time as any.'

'You're crazy,' Fenton said thinly. 'How was I to know Grandfather was out of the house this evening? He only walks in the garden around noon, when the sun is hottest. Helen had been at the house only a couple of minutes before Grandfather appeared. I was down by the gate, and I saw it all happening. I didn't have the time to get from the gate after letting you in, Helen, to the cage where the dog was. That dog forced its own way out, and that's all there is to it.'

'Perhaps it wasn't intended to escape

tonight,' Howard went on implacably. 'You cut those wires at the bottom there, knowing that sooner or later the dog would escape. Don't deny it, Fenton. It's very plain to me.'

'Then report it to the police and see how far you get,' Fenton said. 'This is preposterous, Howard. I don't know what you're trying to prove, but you won't succeed. If you're that keen to get your hands on the estate you'll have to do better than that.'

'I'm not scheming anything of the sort,' Howard retorted. 'You're the type for that, Fenton. But you've gone too far. I'm going to telephone for the police, and you'd better know what you're going to tell them when they get here.'

'You damned fool!' Fenton's expression changed, and Helen clearly saw the ugliness in his dark eyes. 'You're not going to get your hands on the estate. It's mine by right of birth. My father was the eldest son. If he'd lived to inherit, then I would have been next in line for it. Damn you, Howard. You've lived here as long as I have, but you've always been on the inside with the old man. He never liked me because he thought I was insane like my mother.'

'There's no need to talk to me about it,' Howard said firmly. 'Save your explanations for the police. If Grandfather dies of shock you'll have a lot to answer for. Now lock that dog in that empty cage along there, and come up to the house with me.'

Fenton stared at them, his dark eyes filled with anger and frustration. Helen felt a coldness enveloping her. There was madness in Fenton's face at this moment.

'Do as I say,' Howard went on harshly. 'If you set that dog on us I'll shoot it. Get it in a cage and be quick about it. I'm not fooling, Fenton. This has gone far enough. I want to get to the bottom of this.'

Fenton turned slowly and took the dog along the line of cages, halting at an empty one, and he put the animal inside, bolting the door. Helen sighed her relief and relaxed a little. Howard did not move.

'You'd better come up to the house with us,' he ordered.

'I shall stay here,' Fenton replied. 'I'm not guilty of anything, and I'm certainly not going to run away. I have some work to do here, and if you are sending for the police, then I shall be here when they arrive. Now get out of my sight.'

Howard walked forward and picked up the remains of his grandfather's deerstalker, then turned towards the house, and Helen went with him. Howard kept a careful watch over his shoulder as they left the cages, and Helen did the same. She didn't want to leave anything to chance. If Fenton suddenly turned another dog loose there would be another dreadful scene. She shuddered as she recalled the tense moment when Edsel Ormond was being attacked.

When they entered the house Howard bolted the door, and Helen glanced at him.

'I'm not taking any chances,' he said grimly. 'Fenton looked capable of anything when we left him. I'm certain it did happen as we've worked it out. He deliberately got that dog aroused, and he cut that wire. He knew the dog would find the weak spot in time and get loose, and it was obvious that having got loose, the dog would attack Grandfather at the first opportunity. Go and bolt the front door, Helen, while I call the police. I want Fenton questioned and those dogs removed this evening.'

'You don't think he might turn the rest of the animals loose, and set them on to us?' Helen demanded.

'Would you put it past him?' Howard demanded.

'I don't think so,' she said slowly, and hurried to bolt the front door. When she walked into the library Howard was using the telephone, and she listened to his words, almost unable to believe them.

'The police will be here shortly,'

Howard said, replacing the telephone. 'We're going to stay here in the house until they arrive. I've warned them about the dogs, so they'll know what to expect. Come on, let's go up into one of the back bedrooms and watch the rear of the house. We'll be able to see those cages from the top floor.'

Helen followed him through the house, and they ascended the rear stairs, entering a small bedroom and crossing to the window. When they peered out they could see the cages well enough, but there was no sign of Fenton, and Helen felt a cold shiver of fear inside her when she noticed that half the cages were now empty.

'Howard,' she cried in vibrant tones. 'The dogs are gone out of the cages.'

'So I see!' Howard was tense. 'Where the devil is Fenton, and what is he up to?'

'You don't really think he'd let those animals loose on us, do you?'

'We're perfectly safe in the house, I should think,' he said slowly. 'But let's get up into the attic. We can see beyond the back yard. Perhaps Fenton is turning the dogs loose into that paddock he uses.'

They went to the door, and as Howard opened it the sound of a scream echoed through the lower part of the house. Helen stiffened in sudden fear, and Howard put out a hand to prevent her leaving the room. There was the sound of sudden and ferocious barking down below, and a door slammed quickly. Then Fenton's voice was heard urging on the dogs, and paws thudded on the stairs, and in the background there was the sound of opening and closing doors.

Howard went outside into the corridor and peered over the stairs. Helen stood in the doorway of the room, wondering what would happen next, and she moved back into the room as Howard wheeled and sprinted towards her.

'The dogs are coming up the stairs,' he said in breathless tones, slamming the door and bolting it. Fenton is behind them. He's got a whip and he's urging them on. He means to turn those animals loose on us, Helen.'

Helen looked at the door. It was thick and solid, and looked as if it could withstand a siege.

'I think we're safe in here,' Howard said thinly. 'But let's move that furniture over here and block up the doorway, just in case. I wish I hadn't left that shotgun downstairs.'

They moved quickly to do as he suggested, and before they could move any of the furniture they heard the sound of scratching on the outside of the door. Then there was a concert of barking and growling. Heavy bodies hurled themselves savagely at the door, and Helen put a hand to her mouth as her imagination worked overtime.

'Howard,' she said fearfully, and he put a bandaged hand on her shoulder.

'Don't worry, darling,' he said resolutely. 'They can't get through that door.'

'But if Fenton is outside he may try

to break it down.'

Before Howard could reply they heard Fenton's voice out there in the corridor, and he was shouting the dogs and cracking a whip. By degrees the turmoil of dogs outside the door lessened, and Fenton shouted in thick, almost unrecognisable tones.

'Howard, I know you're in there,' he said. 'So you think you've won out, do you? Well you won't be so happy when these dogs get at you. You'll be dead by the time the police get here, and so will your precious doctor. You're not getting anything. You want the estate and the girl, and I wanted them both. But if I can't have them, then you won't either, and that's all there is to it. I turned that dog loose on Grandfather. The silly old fool had cut me out of his will. He wanted it to go the way you did. The estate is yours if you marry Helen. Well I'm going to prevent that ever happening. I'm letting the dogs finish you off. There'll be no evidence against me. I'm the one trying to stop them getting at you. I'll be a hero, and you'll both be dead. I don't suppose Grandfather will survive that mauling he got, and that will leave everything to me. I've been waiting years for Grandfather to die, and I would have got this place if Helen hadn't come along. But it's going my way in the end, and that's all that matters.'

'He's completely unhinged,' Howard said quietly. 'But I don't think he can get through that door, Helen, so don't worry. The police will be here very soon, and they'll take care of him.' He took her arm and led her across to the window. 'I don't know if this is the room, but from one of these back rooms it is possible to get up on to the roof. The dogs wouldn't be able to get at us there.'

A gunshot blasted suddenly, shaking the room, and they both spun to stare at the door. A small hole had appeared in the woodwork near the bolt, and Helen set her teeth into her lip as she watched. Fenton had the gun, and if he had enough cartridges he would be able to shoot the bolt off the door. Then nothing would save them!

But there was a sudden commotion outside the door. Dogs were howling and Fenton was shouting at the top of his voice. The house seemed to shake to another shot, and a dog howled in sudden agony. Howard took Helen in his arms as they listened. There was a sudden yell of terror from Fenton, and then a long cry of pain. The sound of paws thudded on the thinly carpeted floor, and they heard the unmistakable sounds of dogs running down the stairs. Then silence fell, and for a few moments Howard remained like a statue, stiff and filled with fear, holding Helen in his strong grasp. Then he sighed and released her, and she saw determination on his face.

'What are you going to do, Howard?' she demanded.

'I think those dogs turned on Fenton,' he said slowly. 'I'm going to have a look.'

'Oh no! It might be a trick.'

'I don't think so. The dogs have gone

down the stairs. Come and stand behind the door, and be ready to slam it shut if I'm wrong. I must take a look, Helen.'

She nodded, and he kissed her. As they moved across the room Howard put a hand around her shoulders.

'I'll make this up to you when this is all over,' he said. 'There'll be a lot of changes around here, I promise you.'

Helen did not reply. Her teeth were clenched, and she wanted to stop him from opening the door, but Howard reached for the bolt and slid it gently back. He put a toe near the bottom of the door to prevent it being forced open wide, and Helen took a deep breath as he slowly eased the door open a fraction. Howard peered through the crack, and for a moment he was rigid with tension. Helen could hear her heart beating, and a pulse in her throat hurt with its intense throbbing. The sudden silence in the house was heavy and oppressive.

Then Howard opened the door and

peered out into the passage, ready to retreat into the room and slam the door. Helen peered through the crack of the door between the heavy hinges, and her heart seemed to miss a beat when she spotted Fenton lying on his back, the front of his white shirt stained darkly with blood that had gushed from his torn throat. The body of a dog lay near by.

Howard went out and picked up the gun, and he reloaded it with cartridges taken from his pocket. Helen hurried out to the corridor, her fears overwhelmed by the sight of an injured man. She dropped to her knees beside him, but a glance was sufficient to show that Fenton was dead. She checked his pulse and his heart, and there was nothing.

'He's dead!' She got to her feet and faced Howard, who was looking towards the stairs.

'Stay here,' he commanded. 'I'm going down to clear the house.'

'I'll stick by your side,' Helen said fervently.

'For the rest of our lives,' he added. 'Don't you agree, Helen?'

'For the rest of our lives,' she said happily.

There was a step on the stairs, and they both turned quickly. Lucy was peering at them, and the girl was holding a sporting rifle. For a moment she stared at them, and then looked at the motionless figure of Fenton. Then the girl gave a great sigh and almost tumbled down the stairs in her relief. Helen hurried to her side, holding her.

'The dogs have gone out of the house, Mr Howard,' the girl said breathlessly. 'Mr Fenton brought them in and searched for you down below. I locked myself in a cupboard in the kitchen, and stayed there until they came here. Then I sneaked out to get this gun, and I opened the front and back doors. I heard two shots up here, and was afraid that you'd been killed. The dogs all came running down the stairs and went out, so I shut the doors again.'

'You did the right thing, Lucy,' Howard said heavily. 'I don't think there's anything more to fear. The police will be here very shortly and they'll take care of everything. Come on, we'll leave this situation just as it is.'

Lucy preceded them down the stairs, and Helen followed Howard, her heart hammering now like a mad thing. Shock clung thickly to her consciousness, but underneath it all lay a thin layer of happiness, and she breathed deeply as they reached the ground floor. When the sharpness of this evening's dreadful events had faded there would be a return to the pleasant routine into which she and Howard had slipped, but it would never be exactly the same again. Their understanding of one another had been extended by this tragedy, and all uncertainties had fled. It was as if a tiny spark was flickering into life within her, and it would engulf Howard with its fire and brilliance, welding him to her, lighting up their future with happiness and promise . . .

We do hope that you have enjoyed reading this large print book.

Did you know that all of our titles are available for purchase?

We publish a wide range of high quality large print books including:
Romances, Mysteries, Classics
General Fiction
Non Fiction and Westerns

Special interest titles available in large print are:
The Little Oxford Dictionary
Music Book, Song Book
Hymn Book, Service Book

Also available from us courtesy of Oxford University Press:
Young Readers' Dictionary
(large print edition)
Young Readers' Thesaurus
(large print edition)

For further information or a free brochure, please contact us at:
Ulverscroft Large Print Books Ltd.,
The Green, Bradgate Road, Anstey,
Leicester, LE7 7FU, England.
Tel: (00 44) **0116 236 4325**
Fax: (00 44) **0116 234 0205**

GIRL ON THE RUN

Rhonda Baxter

A job in a patent law firm is a far cry from the glamorous existence of a pop star's girlfriend. But it's just what Jane Porter needs to distance herself from her cheating ex and the ensuing press furore. In a new city with a new look, Jane sets about rebuilding her confidence — something she intends to do alone. That is, until she meets patent lawyer Marshall Winfield. But with the paparazzi still hot on Jane's heels, and an office troublemaker hell-bent on making things difficult, can they find happiness together?

FRESH STARTS AT FOLLY FARM

Sharon Booth

Rachel and her son Sam have moved back to the farm where she grew up — now a shadow of its former self, all livestock gone. Then a horse appears in the stables overnight! The culprit is Xander, an actor seeking an anonymous holiday in Bramblewick, who has rescued the horse from his cruel owner. Soon word gets around that Folly Farm is taking in old and unwanted animals, and the menagerie grows — as does the mutual attraction between Rachel and Xander . . .

CASE NURSE

Phyllis Mallett

When Karen Gregory arrives at Glen Hall to nurse the elderly matriarch of the Murrays, the desolate surroundings immediately dampen her spirits. Mrs Murray's sons are at odds with the housekeeper; and the younger one, Roy, introduces himself to Karen with a kiss! Then an injury which might not be accidental sends the older son, Duncan, to hospital; a situation that ultimately results in Karen being ordered to leave the Hall. But she's determined to help — and she's already fallen in love with one of the handsome brothers . . .

COMING HOME

Zara Thorne

Holly Engleby never imagined she'd return to Charnley Acre with only half her university course completed — and a baby on the way. Moving into a house share, she finds a job and settles back into village life. But Holly has growing feelings for Isaac, the owner of the house — and what should she do about the baby? As autumn approaches, she faces the most heart-breaking decision of her life. Is she destined to live in the shadow of her past mistakes, and deny herself the chance of love with Isaac?

A MOST DELIGHTFUL CHRISTMAS

Fenella J. Miller

Richard Finchley holds a Christmas house party at his home in order to find his cousin, the Earl of Abingdon, a wife. When Freddie and Lucy Halston discover that their father has made a bid for the earl and that they will therefore be attending the party, they hatch a scheme to behave as deplorably as they can, so as to escape unwanted marital ties to a stranger. However, it is Richard who unexpectedly falls for Freddie's unconventional charms, and who she must therefore discourage . . .